Stranger Than Science

BY FRANK EDWARDS

My First 10,000,000 *Sponsors*
Strangest of All

By FRANK EDWARDS

STRANGER THAN SCIENCE

CITADEL PRESS   SECAUCUS, N.J

To Candy, a devoted friend

Table of Contents

PART TWO

Table of Contents

Introduction

Much of the material in this book has come from my syndicated radio program "Stranger Than Science" which is now heard throughout most of the English-speaking world.

Gathering the material was a labor of love over a period of at least thirty years and I hereby wish to express my profound thanks to those who helped: the research staff at the Library of Congress and the National Archives; the assistant editors at National Geographic Society; the many librarians in scattered institutions who took the time to find and report the answers to my questions, and especially do I wish to thank Curtis and Mary Fuller for the invaluable permission to use the files of FATE magazine.

None of the incidents reported herein is subject to rational explanation by conventional means. They are all documented examples of the impossible, contradicting orthodox science by their very existence, unexplained and unexplainable. Their very existence indicates clearly that the five senses of man are not capable of detecting all that goes on about him, and that science has by no means acquired a working knowledge of some powerful forces that are unmistakably real, although thus far unidentified.

11

It would be a mistake to twit science for its inability to understand these things, for science itself is a comparative youngster. Organized, systematic scientific research hardly existed before 1875. Since then it has made remarkable progress but, as the material in this book will show, there is still much unexplored territory. The late Thomas Edison once said of a frustrating series of experiments: "They taught us a lot we hadn't known before and they also taught us how little we understand about some of the things we did know."

Thanks to science, Man is now preparing to leave an earth whose forces he little understands to journey into a cosmos which he understands not at all. It is a venture which should give us a better appreciation of our modest intellectual attainments on earth and a magnificent conception of our colossal ignorance of the universe.

By presenting these stories in printed form I must admit to another and more mundane purpose; I hope to solve the mystery of whether an author can make money out of a book like this. Trusting that you and fifty thousand of your friends will accord me the joys of an affirmative reply, I remain

Sincerely yours,
FRANK EDWARDS

PART
ONE

1

The Mystery of David Lang

Is it possible for a human being to literally walk off the earth in full view of witnesses? Before you answer, I suggest that we consider the case of David Lang.

It happened in the twinkling of an eye on a bright sunshiny afternoon. The date was September 23, 1880. The place was the farm of David Lang, a few miles from Gallatin, Tennessee.

Fate had set the scene of this tragic mystery in pleasing surroundings. Lang's home was a rambling brick house almost covered with vines. Before it lay a forty-acre pasture, cropped close by the cattle, that was now browned by the long summer dry spell which had not yet come to an end.

On that particular afternoon, Lang's two children, George, eight, and his daughter, eleven-year-old Sarah, were playing with a new wooden wagon pulled by wooden horses, a toy their father had brought back from Nashville that morning. The youngsters were pulling the toy around in the front yard as their mother and father came out of the house.

Mrs. Lang said to her husband, "Hurry back, Dave. I

want you to drive me into town before the stores close." Mr. Lang by now had reached the fence on his way across the pasture to see his beautiful quarter horses, of which he was understandably proud. He stopped at the fence to look at his big pocket watch. With a wave of the hand he said, "I'll be back in just a few minutes."

But he never came back; for David Lang was only thirty seconds from his rendezvous with fate, whatever it was!

The youngsters spotted a horse and buggy coming up the long lane toward the house, and stopped their play to watch it; for they recognized it as the conveyance of Judge August Peck, who always had presents for them. Mrs. Lang saw the carriage, as did David, for he waved at the Judge and turned to come back to the house.

David Lang had not taken more than half a dozen steps when he disappeared in full view of all those present. Mrs. Lang screamed. The children, too startled to realize what had happened, stood mutely. Instinctively, they all ran toward the spot where Lang had last been seen a few seconds before. Judge Peck and his companion, the Judge's brother-in-law, scrambled out of their buggy and raced across the field. The five of them arrived on the spot of Lang's disappearance almost simultaneously. There was not a tree, not a bush, not a hole to mar the surface. And not a single clue to indicate what had happened to David Lang.

The grownups searched the field around and around, and found nothing. Mrs. Lang became hysterical and had to be led screaming into the house. Meanwhile, neighbors had been alerted by the frantic ringing of a huge bell that stood in the side yard, and they spread the alarm. By nightfall scores of people were on the scene, many of them with lanterns. They searched every foot of the field in which

Lang had last been seen a few hours before. They stamped their feet on the dry hard sod in hope of detecting some hole into which he might have fallen—but they found none.

David Lang was gone. He had vanished in full view of his wife, his two children, and the two men in the buggy. One second he was there, walking across the sunlit field, the next instant he was gone.

In the weeks that followed, authorities had to take steps to keep curiosity seekers away from the farm. Mrs. Lang was bedridden from the shock of the experience. All the servants left with the exception of the old family cook, Sukie, and, thanks to Judge Peck, some measure of peace and quiet was restored.

Subsequent examination of the witnesses disclosed that they had all seen the same thing at the same time and place. The county surveyor probed the field where Lang had vanished, and found it to be solidly supported by a thick layer of limestone, without sinkholes or caves. There was never a funeral, nor even a memorial service for Mr. Lang. His wife, who lived many years after the event, clung to the hope that somehow, sometime, David Lang would return.

Eventually, she let Judge Peck rent out the farm, with the exception of the field in front of the house. That pasture she left untouched as long as she lived.

With the passage of time, the excitement which followed the remarkable disappearance of David Lang subsided. Winter came, and spring again. Mrs. Lang had sold her horses, so Judge Peck pastured his own horses in the field.

As strange as the disappearance itself was the experience which befell Lang's two youngsters one still warm evening in April of 1881, about seven months after he had vanished.

17

The children noticed that at the spot where he had last been seen, there was a circle of stunted yellow grass some fifteen feet in diameter. On that evening as they stood beside the circle, eleven-year-old Sarah called to their father; and, to their astonishment, the youngsters heard his voice . . . calling faintly for help . . . over and over . . . until it faded away, forever.

2

The Abominable Snowman

Sneering at natives' tales of incredible monsters isn't wise . . . for sometimes the natives know whereof they speak. This was clearly demonstrated in the latter half of the 19th century when an American explorer, Paul Du Chailliu, brought home the skin and skeleton of a giant gorilla to confound his critics.

Thus far no one has brought in hide nor hair of the Abominable Snowman of the Himalayas but there are scientists who expect this to happen at any time.

The natives who live in that stark, forbidding, region call these creatures yeti . . . which we have translated into Abominable. That isn't the real meaning of the word, but it's the nearest thing we can use for general distribution in mixed company. The yeti, or Abominable Snowmen, according to the natives, live high in the craggy fastnesses of the Himalayas . . . a reservation which no one covets. But the trouble is that they come down into the valleys where the natives live, upon occasion. And according to the stories told by the pop-eyed Sherpas, the yeti do not confine themselves to eating frogs from the valley ponds . . . and tender shoots from the trees and rice patches. They also indulge themselves in a craving for fresh meat . . . sometimes stealing a goat . . . sometimes stealing a pet yak . . . and sometimes making off with a child or an isolated herdsman who made the fatal error of sleeping in the sun.

As the British occupation of India spread to the foothills of the awesome Himalayas, they encountered their first reports of these strange creatures . . . and dismissed them as figments of overwrought native imaginations. The first tiny crack in the wall of doubt came in 1913 when a group of Chinese hunters wounded and captured a strange manlike creature which the Tibetans called a snowman.

The Chinese said that it was kept captive at Patang in Sinkiang province for months, a creature with a black monkey-like face, covered with silvery yellow hair several inches long. It had exceptionally powerful hands and had feet much like those of a human, rather than an ape. It grunted and made guttural sounds but spent most of its time pursing its lips and making loud whistling noises. After about five months, it sickened and died.

The outbreak of World War One stifled any scientific ventures into that area. In 1937, a British explorer, Frank Smythe, came out of Tibet with reports of manlike wild creatures of an unknown type which frequented the upper reaches of the Himalayas, living on grubs and rodents and on larger animals when they could get them.

Smythe had found their tracks at the 14,000-foot level; his Sherpa guides took one look and refused to go on.

Measurement of the prints showed that they were remarkably human in shape . . . but the stride was such that one foot imprinted its toes in the heel mark of the other. . . . Size: about thirteen inches long by five inches wide.

Since that time many expeditions have reported finding evidence that the Abominable Snowman is a living creature which may some day be brought into camp.

Some have seen no more than a British Major, Alan Cameron, who was with the Everest Expedition of 1923. He and his party were working their way toward the peak of Everest when one of the guides spotted a line of living creatures moving slowly along a cliff face well above the snow line. Two days later, when Cameron's group reached a point near that cliff face they found giant, manlike footprints in the snow. . . .

In late 1936, the first Shipton Expedition to Everest encountered more of the strange tracks where there should have been no tracks . . . around the fringes of the snow line on the bleak slopes of the approaches to Everest. H. W. Tilman, a member of the Shipton expedition who followed the tracks for several miles, noted that they ran one behind the other in a manner no four-footed creature uses. Tilman finally lost them on a long stretch of barren rock.

In 1958 an American scientist, Dr. Norman Dyrenfurth, reported from Katmandu, Nepal, that he had found evidence which convinced him that the Abominable Snowmen were in reality a very low grade of human or near human creatures. By seeking out caves in which they had lived without fire, he collected hair, both silver-grey and reddish-brown, food scraps, plastercasts of footprints and other odds and ends to show that the elusive snowmen are real . . . and that they are of two species . . . the large one about eight feet tall at maturity . . . the other about four feet tall.

Also in 1958 an anthropologist at Johns Hopkins declared that the Abominable Snowman footprints were prints made by natives whose toes stuck thru their worn out sandals . . . to which the Chicago Tribune replied, "It's a good explanation for one who has never been there . . . and who lives far enough away to be disinterested!"

21

3

Neglected Genius

Years before Marconi won fame for sending and receiving wireless code signals, a Kentucky farmer had been publicly sending and receiving both voice and music by wireless. His success is no stranger than the oblivion that befell him.

The crowd that milled around on the court house lawn in Murray, Kentucky, on that memorable day in 1892 had no concept of the historic nature of the occasion. They had come by the hundreds to scoff at the efforts of an eccentric fellow farmer named Nathan Stubblefield, who claimed that he could send messages through the air without wires. Even when he performed the feat before their own senses, they failed to appreciate the magnitude of the event.

At points about two hundred feet apart on the court house lawn Stubblefield had set up two boxes, each about two feet square, and not connected in any way. Each box contained a telephone—and as Stubblefield and his son talked to each other from opposite sides of the court house lawn their voices could be clearly heard by the curious crowd that clustered around the boxes.

When the historic experiment was concluded, Stubblefield was greeted by hoots and snickers. He angrily gathered up his equipment and tossed it into his wagon, condemning himself for his stupidity in conducting the demonstration among such dolts.

It was 1892. Marconi, later to become famous as the father of wireless, was then just an eighteen-year-old boy. Nathan Stubblefield, telephone fixer, who eked out an existence on a flinty farm in Calloway County, Kentucky, had conducted a public demonstration of wireless transmission of the human voice for the first time in history—and had been hooted out of town for his achievement.

Word of what he had done finally reached the St. Louis Post Dispatch, which wrote to him asking for a demonstration. Weeks later the paper received acknowledgment of their request—a post card which said simply: "Have accepted your invitation. Come to my place any time. Nathan Stubblefield, inventor." The reporter for the Post Dispatch arrived at Stubblefield's little farm on January 10, 1902. The inventor handed him a telephone which was connected to a pair of steel rods about four feet long, and told him to take the outfit anywhere he liked in that neighborhood, stick the rods into the earth, and put the receiver to his ear.

In recounting his experience, in the newspaper article, the reporter told how he had gone about a mile from the inventor's house, jabbed the rods into the earth, and, as he said, "I could hear every syllable the Stubblefield boy spoke into a transmitter as clearly as if he were just across the room!"

How did he do it? Stubblefield told the newsman that he was merely using the electrical field which permeated the earth, the water, and the atmosphere. He predicted that some day wireless transmission of speech would enable people living in Kentucky to listen to weather reports from

23

the nation's capitol, and to hear music and news from points all over the world.

The newspaper article brought invitations for this Kentucky telephone repairman and part-time farmer to bring his gear to Philadelphia for demonstration before interested financiers. Stubblefield scored a spectacular success there in May of 1902, and then went on to Washington, D. C., where he again amazed the scientists of his time by the magic of his abilities.

As usual, the skeptics were on hand to see him fail. It was preposterous to expect this untutored fellow from the Kentucky hills to send and receive voice messages when Marconi himself could only send and receive dot and dash code.

The gear was installed on the little steamship, Bartholdi, and scores of prominent persons stationed themselves at points of their own choosing along the Virginia shore of the Potomac. As the ship churned the waters, the startled dignitaries communicated with those aboard the vessel, clearly and distinctly, by merely sticking the customary iron rods in the ground and speaking into their telephones.

The Washington Evening Star said in headlines on May 21, 1902: — "First Practical Test of Wireless Telegraphy Heard For Half Mile. Invention of Kentucky Farmer. Wireless telephony demonstrated beyond question."

Plaudits ringing in his ears, financiers begging him for contracts to enable them to develop the invention, Stubblefield packed up his gear and went home. He was afraid someone would steal his ideas. He took out patents, but they make little sense to those who have studied them.

As time dragged by and others learned to send voice messages just as he had done years before, Stubblefield became increasingly bitter and morose. He was found dead in his crude shack in the spring of 1929, his equipment missing, his records scattered.

A stone memorial on the court house lawn at Murray, Kentucky, marks the spot where he made history in 1892. He had foreseen with surprising accuracy the wonders that broadcasting would accomplish—and he said of himself with undeniable accuracy—"I have lived fifty years before my time!"

4

A Modern Jonah

Is it possible for a man to be swallowed by a whale and live to tell the story? The "scientific" answer is NO—but the correct answer is YES—.

The official records of the British Admiralty provide documentary evidence for the astounding account of James Bartley, a British seaman who was swallowed by a whale—and lived to tell about it!

James was making his first and only trip as a sailor aboard the whaling ship Star of the East. In February of 1891 she was pounding along before a fair wind a few hundred miles east of the Falkland Islands, in the South Atlantic.

Suddenly the lookout gave his electrifying cry of "there she blows!" . . . for he had sighted a huge sperm whale half a mile off the port bow. The Star of the East slackened her sails and the whaling crews scrambled into their three small boats, off to harpoon the mighty mammal if possible.

Young James Bartley was in the first longboat to reach the side of the whale. Pulling slowly on their oars, the sailors drove their frail cockleshell behind the unsuspecting creature, so near that the harpooner could lean over and drive his huge spear deep into the whale's vitals Bartley and his fellow seamen backed frantically to get out of the reach of those massive tail flukes which threshed the water to foam as the stricken beast fought to free itself of the barbed harpoon.

For a moment, luck seemed to be with the sailors. The whale plunged deep into the ocean, and eight hundred feet of heavy line streaked out of the tub before the creature ceased to dive. . . . Then there was an ominous slackening in the line—the great brute was coming up—but where? In such cases this was a matter of life and death—and the sailors did not have long to wait for the answer. They hunched over their oars, ready to pull for their lives once they knew which way to pull.

Without warning, the sea boiled ᵤp around them—there was a splintering crash . ᵤᵣ ᵣail boat spun into the air. The mortally wounded whale threshed about madly in his agony—beating the water to a bloody froth before he sounded to the depths again.

A nearby longboat picked up the survivors—but two men were missing, one of them the apprentice sailor, James Bartley.

The wind which had borne the Star of the East to the scene of this tragedy now deserted her and she wallowed in the long swells, her sails flapping.

Shortly before sunset on that same fateful day, the dying whale floated to the surface about four hundred yards from the vessel. The crew hastily fastened a line to the whale, and the winch brought it slowly to the ship. Hot weather made it imperative that it be cut up at once. Since they had no means of raising the hundred-ton mammal to the deck, the men took flensing spades and peeled off the thick blubber as they slipped and slid along the creature's back. Dirty work . . . and dangerous . . . for the water was full of sharks maddened by the taste of blood.

Shortly before eleven that night, working by lantern light, the tired crewmen removed the stomach and the huge liver, and hoisted them aboard ship for processing. There on deck they were startled to notice movement inside the giant paunch . . . a slow rhythmic movement that looked like something breathing.

The captain hurriedly called the ship's doctor, and a great incision was made in the tough flesh. . . . A human foot became visible . . . shoe and all! A moment later they had pulled out one of the missing sailors . . . it was James Bartley . . . doubled up . . . unconscious . . . but alive!

Perhaps for want of anything better, the excited doctor ordered Bartley drenched with buckets of sea water . . . a treatment which soon restored consciousness, but not reason. Bartley was babbling incoherently as he threshed about in his delirium. For almost two weeks he lingered between life and death, strapped to the bunk in the captain's cabin. Gradually, so the ship's doctor wrote in the record which was signed by all on board, Bartley recovered his senses, but it was a month before he was able to tell what had happened.

He remembered being flung into the air when the whale crushed their longboat, and as he fell back into the sea he saw the tremendous mouth open over him. He screamed as he was engulfed. There were sharp stabbing pains as he swept across the rows of tiny sharp teeth. Then he found himself sliding down a slimy tube . . . he could recall fighting for his breath . . . kicking about . . . then blissful oblivion . . . until he regained consciousness a month later in the captain's cabin.

A Modern Jonah

He had been inside the whale's stomach for fifteen hours, and as a result he lost all the hair on his body, his skin was bleached to an unnatural whiteness, and he was almost blind for the rest of his life, which he spent as a shoe cobbler in his native Gloucester.

Numerous medical men from many lands came to examine him and to discuss his incredible experience. He lived eighteen years after his adventure, and on his tombstone is a brief account of his experience, and a footnote which says . . . "James Bartley—1870 - 1909 . . . a modern Jonah."

5

Famous Last Words

A Roman soldier brandished his short two-handed sword menacingly around the head of the old man seated on the floor. Archimedes, one of the greatest of early Greek scholars, never bothered to look up. The soldier ordered the old man to rise and follow him. Said Archimedes, "No. Not until I have finished my problem!" A moment later the sword in the hands of a nameless soldier brought an end to the career of one of the greatest thinkers of all time.

Henry Ward Beecher, stormy and controversial pulpit figure of the mid-nineteenth century, had preached to millions during his lifetime. He had counselled them to be ready for the Grim Reaper and he had pictured for them what lay beyond the grave. As Beecher himself lay gasping out his last breath, he pulled the physician down to him and whispered hoarsely, "Doctor, now comes the mystery!"

Ann Boleyn, consort of the King, was ready to pay with her life for her involvement with royalty. She was calm to the last. Turning to a companion who was trembling violently, Ann said: "Take courage. The executioner is an expert of many years' training . . . and my neck is very slender."

Outside the bedchamber of Queen Elizabeth, scores of

persons knelt to pray for her. The Queen, attended by the finest physicians of the time, was struggling to the last. As the Pale Horseman drew nearer and nearer she could no longer deny the inevitable to herself. Shaking a clenched fist at her own impotence, she said, "All my possessions for one moment of time!"

Cardinal Wolsey, like many another who aspired to greatness, became entangled in the political toils of his time and paid for it with his life. As he faced the executioner. . . . "Had I but served my God with but half the zeal that I served my king, He would not have left me in my gray hairs!"

William Porter, known to millions for his delightful short stories written under the name of O. Henry, was ill for a long time before he realized that the end was near. He clutched the hand of a close friend who sat beside his bed. For a long minute there was no sound except his labored breathing. Then at last the famous writer said, "Charlie—I'm afraid to go home in the dark!"

Sir Thomas More was being led to the scaffold blindfolded. He asked that the bandage be removed and to his jailer he remarked, "See me safely up to the gibbet, sir! On the downward voyage let me shift for myself."

John Barrymore was another whose sense of humor was with him to the last. He had been unconscious and near death for hours when he suddenly regained consciousness. With his last bit of strength, he managed a faint puckish grin as he said to his friend Gene Fowler . . . "Tell me, Gene . . . are you really the illegitimate son of Buffalo Bill?"

Doctor Samuel Garth, famous physician who had made a fortune ministering to the ailments of Renaissance royalty, had one last request to make of the fellow physicians who gathered round his bedside. "Please, gentlemen," he said "stand back and let me die a natural death!"

And Hobbes, consultant to the great and near great of his day, said, "I go now to take my last voyage . . . a leap in the dark!"

The Countess of Rouen was famed for her impeccable manners. As the end for her drew near, a servant tiptoed into the room and announced that a visitor wished to see the Countess. The courteous lady had the servant write a card which said, "The Countess of Rouen sends her compliments but begs to be excused. She is engaged in dying."

James Smithson, founder of the world-famous Smithsonian Institution in Washington, was a very unusual man in many ways and he had a knack for wry humor that was with him to the last. His fatal illness was one which the doctors had not been able to diagnose. When he realized that little time was left, he called his physicians to him and said: "I want you to perform an autopsy to discover what is wrong with me. I'm dying for you to find out what it is!"

Thomas Edison's last remark left a puzzled family. The great inventor was not an atheist, as some have claimed—neither did he discuss his beliefs, whatever they were, with those nearest to him. As Edison lay dying, slowly and painfully, his wife held his hand. He seemed to be asleep. Other than the labored beating of his heart, the room was perfectly quiet.

Suddenly Mr. Edison sat up in bed without assistance. He opened his eyes and stared straight ahead for several seconds. Then he turned to Mrs. Edison and said, "I am surprised! It is very beautiful over there!"

What did he see?

Mr. Edison did not say . . . and no man can tell us.

6

The Devil's
Footprints

The good citizens of Canvey Island had never seen anything like it and they were disturbed, so they dragged the creature out of the shallow water along the beach, covered it with seaweed and ran for the authorities.

The authorities sent for help, too, and the British government assigned the task to a pair of competent zoologists. These gentlemen examined the fantastic creature at length, photographed it, and finally admitted that it looked like nothing they had ever seen before.

It appeared to be some sort of marine creature — but it had feet and legs so arranged that it could walk if it chose. In an upright stance it would have been about two-and-a-half feet tall, with a thick, brownish-red skin, a pulpy head with two protruding eyes. The scientists measured and photographed . . . and gave up. They had the thing cremated and left without making any public conclusions.

If these learned gentlemen thought they were ending the enigma of Canvey Island once and for all by that simple procedure, they reckoned without the facts — for the case did not end there.

On August 11, 1954, the Reverend Joseph Overs was strolling along the beach of Canvey Island, a couple of

33

miles from the scene of the earlier monster, when he, too, came upon a grotesque carcass wallowing in a small tidal pool. The good man took one look and sent one of his youngsters for the police. The Bobbies pulled the carcass ashore and sent for the experts again.

The creature which had been found in the preceding November had been about two-and-a-half feet tall. This later one was slightly more than four feet in length, weighed about twenty-five pounds, and was in good condition for examination. The report which the perplexed scientists submitted to the British government shows that the thing had two large eyes, nostril holes, and a gaping mouth with strong sharp teeth.

It also had gills — but instead of scales it was covered with a pink skin which the experts reported was as tough as the hide of a healthy pig. Perhaps most remarkable of all, this creature, like that of the preceding November, had two short legs with perfect feet, which ended in five tiny toes arranged in a U-shape—with a concave center arch.

If science was able to identify these monstrosities, the report was never disclosed . . . but to many the things brought back memories of that incredible night in February of 1855 when the English countryside around Devonshire had a most remarkable visitor . . . which may or may not have been akin to the strange creatures found a hundred years later on the shores of Canvey Island.

The story was written in the form of little footprints in the smooth blanket of snow that covered the countryside during the night of February 7—a snowfall that ended around eleven o'clock at night. Sometime between the end of the snowfall and the break of day on February 8th, Devonshire had played host to a mysterious visitor . . . something that had scampered, or pranced, or slithered over fences and fields, over walls and housetops . . . leaving an unbroken line of thousands of footprints to mark its passing.

What was it . . . this thing that could travel nimbly up the walls and over the rooftops of decent God-fearing folks while they slept? Where did it come from—and where did it go? Where it came from remains a mystery . . . but where it went was written in the snow . . . from Topsham and Bicton in the north—to Dawles and Totnes in the south . . . a trail more than a hundred miles long.

A baker in Topsham seems to have been the first to take notice of the trail. He saw the strange marks that preceded him to the door of his little shop—but from a point about three feet short of his door the tracks turned sharply right to a five-foot-high brick wall. The baker noticed that the soft curl of the snow atop the wall was disturbed . . . with the same little footprints. He was not disturbed by this oddity . . . that remained for the other residents of the community.

By nightfall the countryside was up in arms . . . for there were many who attributed the tracks to the devil himself. Tiny hoof-shaped marks exactly eight inches apart . . . from Exmouth . . . across fields and housetops . . . to the bay near Powderham Castle . . . only to reappear on the other side of the bay and on to the end of the trail at Totnes, many miles to the south.

The London Times and other newspapers devoted many columns to reporting the strange story of the Devonshire footprints. There were various explanations ascribing the marks to kangaroos, birds, and even a wolf. None of these was acceptable because none of them fitted the facts.

Perplexed experts nervously advanced the theory that

two or three creatures of unknown type had been involved
. . . a theory that was convenient but not convincing unless
you were willing to agree that three unknown creatures
were possessed of the same irresistible urge at the same time
at three different spots on the coast of Devonshire on the
same night . . . and that after romping over the housetops
they fled back into the water, never to be seen again.

Unless, by some strange chance, the monstrosities
washed up on the coast of Canvey Island in 1953 and '54
were a clue. Did these creatures point to a solution to the
riddle of the Devonshire footprints of a century before . . .
or did they merely add new questions to compound the
mystery?

7

The Vanishing Village

There was something creepy about the appearance of the little Eskimo village that lay before him, and trapper Joe Labelle sensed it as he paused to survey the scene. The icy wind that blew off Lake Anjikuni flapped the skins that hung over the gaping doors of the huts. A few battered kayaks were blown up on the beach. No dogs barked, not a single voice broke the silence. Joe asked himself the logical question—where are the people?

It was a very good question on that raw November day in 1930, and it remains unanswered to this day.

For many years Joe had known this friendly little Eskimo village five hundred miles north of the Mounties' base at Churchill. On this fateful day, he had gone miles out of his way across the frozen tundra to spend a few hours with his friends . . . only to be greeted by an ominous silence.

According to his report to the Northwest Mounted Police, Joe stopped at the edge of the village and yelled a greeting. He got no reply of any kind, a most unusual approach to this friendly little community. He opened the caribou skin flap to one of the huts and called again. More silence. A similar experience awaited him at every tent in the village. Very spooky, he said to himself—for there was no one else to whom he could say it. Spooky? Indeed it was! And so it remains.

Joe spent about an hour in the village examining it for some hint as to what might have happened to the missing populace. He found pots of food hanging untouched over fires which had been cold for months. In one hut were some sealskin garments for a small child, the ivory needle still sticking in the garment where the mother had abruptly ceased her mending.

On the beach were three kayaks, including the one which he knew had belonged to the headman of the village. These flimsy craft had been battered and torn by the wave action on the beach, evidence that they had been long neglected.

Both Joe Labelle and the Mounties who investigated after his report found the most puzzling bits of evidence when they looked into the empty huts and tents. There were the Eskimos' prized rifles standing forlornly beside the doors, waiting for masters who never returned. Now in the Far North the rifle is more than a valued possession, it is virtually a life insurance policy. No Eskimo in his right mind would go on a long trip without his rifle—yet, here were the guns . . . and the Eskimos were gone.

What about the dogs—the big powerful brutes which were almost as important in that bleak land as the rifles?

About a hundred yards from the camp, Labelle and the Mounties found seven dogs. They had been tied to the stumps of some scrubby trees and all had died of starvation, as Canadian pathologists later confirmed.

But the most baffling aspect of the entire enigma was found on the side of the camp opposite the bodies of the dogs. There the Eskimos had buried some member of their tribe under the customary cairn of stones. But this grave had been opened, the body removed—and the stones carefully stacked in two neat piles. Grave robbing is unthinkable to Eskimos—and animals could not have stacked the stones.

The experts summoned by the Mounties spent two weeks examining every bit of evidence they could find at the deserted village. They came to the conclusion that the Eskimos had not been there for about two months when Joe Labelle arrived. This decision was based on the type of berries found in some of the cooking pots.

Evidently the village of about thirty inhabitants had been pursuing its normal way of life when for some reason they all rushed out of their huts and none of them ever got back from whatever had attracted their attention. For reasons unknown the inhabitants of the village—men, women, and children—had left it, willingly or otherwise, in the dead of early winter. They had left so hurriedly they had abandoned their food on the fires, their prized guns, their dogs, their clothing. Skilled trackers failed to find any trail if they had fled over the tundra. The presence of their battered kayaks was mute evidence that they had not ventured out into the lake. And the plundered grave was just another bit of unexplained mystery.

Months of patient and far-flung investigation failed to produce a single trace of any member who had lived in the deserted village of Anjikuni. The Mounted Police filed it as unsolved . . . and so it remains.

8

Living Fossils

Living creatures embedded in solid stone? Science says it can't happen . . . but the evidence indicates that it does . . . and more frequently than most people are aware.

The date—April 22, 1881. Joe Molino was at the sixty-foot level of the Wide West Mine near Ruby Hill, Nevada. He drove his pick under the jagged bit of stone that protruded from the side of the tunnel and pulled it loose. As the stone fell it struck Joe on the foot, and that infuriated him so much that he grabbed a sledge and smashed the offending rock. He was astounded to see a cavity about the size of his fist exposed by the hammer blow, a cavity in the solid rock, and it was filled with white worms of some sort. Joe picked them up. They showed no signs of life at first . . . but after half an hour a few of them began to move . . . and within an hour, as the half dozen miners watched in amazement, the worms were crawling slowly around on the floor of the tunnel. The mine operators took charge of the worms and the stone, sent them to the U. S. Bureau of Mines, and received a letter some weeks later informing them that it was all a misunderstanding; since it could not have happened as the miners had described the circumstances!

Fully as inexplicable was the case of the dull, reddish-gray beetle found entombed in a tight-fitting mould of iron ore taken from the famed Longfellow Mine near Clifton, Arizona, in 1892. When the lump of ore broke and the beetle was discovered in its iron sarcophagus, the sample was turned over to a geologist in El Paso, Mr. Z. T. White. He placed it on a piece of paper in a specimen case that stood in his library, and there, about a week after the thing had been removed from the mine, he detected a movement in the beetle.

Examining it under a magnifying glass, White saw a small beetle slowly emerge from the body of the specimen. Witnesses were hastily summoned. The young beetle was placed in a jar where it lived for several months. Eventually the ore, the beetle encased in it, and the young beetle which had emerged, were turned over to the Smithsonian Institution in Washington, which could only join the others in bewilderment at the evidence.

At the Black Diamond Coal Mine on Mount Diablo, near San Francisco, in 1873, miners discovered a large frog partially embedded in the face of a limestone layer they had just blasted. The frog fitted tightly into his stony crypt; in fact, when he was carefully removed, the stone showed the imprint of his body. Both frog and surroundings were brought to the surface, where the frog lived about a day, evidently blind and only able to move one leg slowly. When the creature died, he and his age-old tomb were presented to the San Francisco Academy of Sciences, visible refutation of the scientific assertion that such things cannot happen.

The living fossils turn up in the oddest places. For instance—the Brown and Hall Sawmill at Acton, Ontario, was sawing up a huge pine log in October, 1893. The outside slabs had been removed and the next slice of the huge circle-saw exposed a dark spot on the wood. The workmen stopped the saw lest the dark spot turn out to be some piece of metal embedded in the wood—and ruinous to costly saw blades. But instead of metal, they had merely taken a thin slice off the outside of a four-inch cavity, from which the head of a live toad now emerged, a toad that had barely escaped being cut in two by the sawteeth. The cavity in which the creature had been trapped was perfectly smooth and almost spherical in shape, as though the toad had been scrambling in it. The tree itself was about 200 years old, and that particular section was some sixty feet above the ground. Before the saw finally freed it, the toad had been surrounded by solid wood about thirty inches thick.

There are many records of living toads cropping out in strange places, including some which may have been embedded in concrete, but many of these instances are subject to question.

Well documented—and baffling—is the case of the giant blocks of granite removed from the underwater footing of the docks at George's Basin in Liverpool in 1829. One of the blocks had to be cut up to make new steps, and the cutting disclosed a small toad which was liberated by enlarging the hole around it.

The creature lived for a few hours, during which time it tried feebly to rise a few times before it finally sank down to rise no more. The British scientists who examined the toad and the tomb could only shake their heads. There was the evidence, but it clashed with dogma; so it had to be shrugged off—and it was.

9

Captain Seabury's Serpent

Sea serpents are customarily relegated to the realm of fantasy, but only by those who haven't examined the records of the good ship Monongahela, and her incredible catch.

The New Bedford Morning Mercury first published the account in February of 1853, just about a year after it had happened.

The record says that Captain Seabury, a veteran of many voyages, was in command of the sailing vessel, Monongahela, on that fateful morning of January 13, 1852, when the lookout called the Captain's attention to something unusual in the water half a mile off the port bow. The vessel was wallowing along slowly in the tantalizing zephyrs of the Pacific doldrums. If the creature that had attracted the lookout's attention was a whale, as seemed likely, it would have to be dealt with by the longboats, for the Monongahela had hardly enough forward motion to answer her helm.

Captain Seabury could distinguish little more with his telescope than with the naked eye. He saw only a huge living creature of some sort, writhing slowly in the tepid water, as though in agony. If it were a whale, it was a very sick whale, Seabury reasoned. Possibly it had been harpooned by some other vessel, had escaped, and was now expiring from its ordeal.

The Captain ordered three longboats dispatched to the scene, and Seabury himself was in the first boat, standing in the bow as they pulled alongside the creature. Motioning for the other boats to swing in and attack, Seabury drove the harpoon deep into the huge beast. As they had done so many times before, the crewmen instinctively pulled for their lives to get their boat out of reach of the enraged creature.

An instant later, a huge head ten feet long surged out of the water and lunged at the boats. Two boats were capsized in a matter of seconds. The frightened sailors realized they were dealing with a monster of some sort, but they had little time to ponder that aspect of their plight; they were busy dodging its vicious lashings, and busy fishing their fellow crewmen out of the sea.

The monster sounded. Captain Seabury leaped out of the way as the heavy line streaked out of the tub and over the bow, smoking on the rail as it went. It quickly became evident that there was not enough line to deal with the creature, and Seabury bent on the spare with only seconds to go. That line, too, went over the side as the wounded beast continued its dive; down and down and down until more than a thousand feet of line were out. Then it stopped —whether from reaching bottom or from fatigue, no one could say.

The Monongahela had crept alongside as the struggle progressed, and it picked up both the crewmen and the line. If the thing was still hooked by the harpoon, it gave no sign. Seabury ordered the line made fast, and rowed over to

44

visit Captain Samuel Gavitt on the Rebecca Sims, which had pulled alongside.

Next morning, according to subsequent reports from Captain Gavitt, the Monongahela began taking up the line that ran from her capstan into the deep. They had recovered only about half the line when the great carcass floated to the surface. It was a massive, monstrous thing, unlike anything any of those present had ever seen before.

Longer than the Monongahela (which was more than a hundred feet from stem to stern) the monster had a huge body, about fifty feet in diameter. The long neck, some ten feet thick, supported a head like that of a gigantic alligator, a head ten feet long containing ninety-four teeth in its jaws. The teeth were uniformly about three inches long and hooking backward like those of a snake.

The body of the creature was a brownish gray, with a light stripe about three feet wide running its full length. There were no fins and no legs, so it was assumed by those present that the creature propelled itself by means of its fifteen foot tail, a knobby creation like the back of a sturgeon.

Now that he had his peculiar prize, the Captain had to decide what to do with it. He thought of rendering it as he would a whale. Seabury ordered it pulled alongside the ship, and the flensing spades were brought out; but they soon showed that the creature was just a tough-skinned beast without blubber.

Captain Seabury had his men hack off the huge and grisly head of the monster, and the rest of the carcass was set adrift, after one of the sailors had made a drawing which all aboard signed. The head was put into a huge pickling vat for preservation. Captain Seabury wrote out a report on the appearance and capture of the monstrosity; and gave it to Captain Gavitt for delivery to New Bedford, since the Monongahela was outward bound.

The Captain's account arrived safely and was duly entered into the records, but what happened to the Monongahela and her strange prize will never be known. Years later her name board was found on the shore of Umnak Island, out in the Aleutians, but the fate of the vessel herself, like the monster she encountered, became just another riddle of the sea.

10

Monument To A
Mystery

Near the village of Pavia in Bedford
County, Pennsylvania, there stands a unique stone monument, erected by public subscription to the memory of a
mystery that was never solved.

On the morning of April 24, 1856, Samuel Cox heard
his dog barking excitedly somewhere in the thick forest that
surrounded his little cabin in Spruce Hollow. He picked
up his shotgun and went to see what the dog had treed, but
before he could locate it, the dog had stopped barking.

Sam had been gone about an hour and a half when he
re-entered the clearing where his shack was located. The
dog was there; his wife, Susannah, was there—but where
were his two sons, George, seven, and Joseph, five? The
father thought the youngsters were at home; the mother
thought they had gone into the forest with their father.
The dog, which knew where the lads had gone, could only
bark and dance about aimlessly.

The frightened parents hurried into the dense woods,
calling and listening—without response. Samuel made his
way over the mountain to the home of his nearest neighbors,
and asked them to help. One of the neighbors set out on

horseback to arouse the scattered families for miles around —the others hurried back with Samuel Cox to help him scour the thickets.

By nightfall more than a hundred men and women were engaged in the hunt for the two missing boys. Hour after hour dragged by and the weary searchers came trudging in, empty-handed.

It was a warm night and there was a fair chance that the boys might have survived, provided they had not tumbled into one of the deep, swift creeks that slashed through the valley. At daybreak the search began again, with additional volunteers who had come from many miles to lend a hand. And again the day passed without a trace of the boys. Time was running out.

The search went on for ten days, says The History of Bedford County, and more than a thousand persons combed the mountains. In desperation, the parents asked a dowser to try his hand with a forked stick. He had found water by that method, it was said; perhaps he could find the missing children. Unfortunately, he could not. The stick twisted and turned, but if it showed the path the boys had taken, it failed to lead to the boys themselves. An old woman who had a local reputation as a sort of witch offered to try her bag of tricks; but those, too, came to naught.

In such a climate of excitement it was probably inevitable that gossips would flourish. Rumor spread the story that the parents themselves had killed the children in hope of attracting sympathy and contributions for themselves. Busybodies, with more curiosity than sense, tore up the floor of the little cabin and dug up the yard around the house, in vain.

Twelve miles from the scene of this frenzied activity,

there lived a quiet young farmer named Jacob Dibert. And Mr. Dibert had a dream.

He dreamed that he was alone in the woods, searching for the children whom he had never seen; and, for that matter, he seemed to be in a part of the forest that he had never seen before. Dibert dreamed that he stepped up on a fallen tree, and there before it lay a dead deer. Leaping over the deer he went on down the deer trail and found a child's shoe and beyond that was a beech tree, lying across a stream. Crossing the stream on the fallen tree, he went on over a stony ridge into a ravine through which a small brook trickled; and there, in the semi-circle formed by the roots of a great birch tree, lay the missing boys, dead.

Jacob told his wife about the dream, but they said nothing to anyone else. The next night he dreamed it all over again, and they decided to tell Mrs. Dibert's brother, Harrison Wysong, who was well acquainted with the area in which the boys had disappeared.

Wysong was skeptical of the dream, but he said nothing. He knew where there *was* such a ridge and the creek and the brook; but he regarded it as a wild goose chase. To ease his sister's mind he took Jacob to the edge of the forest and they began their search.

Five minutes later they stepped up on a fallen tree and there lay a dead deer. Beyond it, some eight yards, a child's shoe! Both men began to run . . . they crossed a creek on a fallen beech tree . . . scrambled up the ridge . . . Jacob spotted a giant birch tree with a shattered top . . . and too excited to speak . . . could only point. And he was right; for at the roots of that birch tree they found the bodies of George and Joseph Cox, dead of exposure, just as Jacob Dibert had seen them in his dream.

The boys were buried in Mt. Union Cemetery, May 8, 1856.

On the fiftieth anniversary of the strange event, a monument, paid for by public subscription, was erected near the spot where their bodies had been found. There the monument still stands, a lasting memorial to an unsolved mystery.

11

Do Dreams Come True?

Whether dreams sometimes constitute a preview of the future is a debatable and highly controversial subject. The evidence is there, though agreement is not.

Science itself has profited greatly from the dreams of great men, and of men who became great. Glastonbury Abbey, long lost, was unearthed as the result of a series of surprisingly vivid dreams. The excavation of the ancient city of Mycenae on the island of Crete was the result of a series of premonitory dreams which changed a wealthy young banker of San Francisco into famed archeologist Heinrich Schliemann. Those discoveries and the dreams which preceded them are matters of record, a quality which they share with still another unexplained—and inexplicable—archeological milestone, the translation of the Babylonian tablets from the Temple of Bel.

Dr. Herman Hilprecht, famed Assyriologist at the University of Pennsylvania, was writing a book entitled "Old Babylonian Inscriptions" and he had the manuscript completed, with the exception of two small agate fragments and the inscriptions upon them. They were apparently finger rings, found in the ruins of the Temple of Bel at Nippur. Since they were broken, the inscriptions were incomplete and therefore indecipherable.

The hour was late and Dr. Hilprecht was tired. His wife came in and urged him to discontinue his wearysome struggle with the fragments of inscribed agate, at least for the time being. But the archeologist had promised to have the book ready for the printer the following day, and he felt that it was imperative to decipher these ancient inscriptions. Mrs. Hilprecht went to bed. Her husband turned again to examining those fragments under a magnifying glass. Then he, too, dozed off.

Suddenly, through the magic of dreams, time spun backward. Dr. Hilprecht saw a tall, thin priest of ancient Babylon standing before him, smiling. He seemed to be of middle age and the hot wind from the nearby desert swirled his white robes about him. In a soft clear voice, the priest said in English: "Come with me. I will help you."

Dr. Hilprecht arose to follow his strange visitor, and as he did so he noticed that he was no longer arising from the chair in which he had dozed off in his library, but was getting up from a huge stone step on which he seemed to have been sitting. He and his visitor strolled through a hot dusty street, past occasional great buildings, all of which seemed to be deserted. They came to a building more massive and more impressive than the others, and there they entered a vast dimly lit room.

"Where am I?" Dr. Hilprecht inquired.

"At Nippur, between the Tigris and the Euphrates, in the Temple of Bel, the father of the Gods," the eerie visitor replied.

The archeologist glanced around at the details of the immense room in which they stood. There was enough similarity to the reconstruction by modern science for him to recognize that the phantom priest was telling the truth.

"Can you tell me where the lost treasure room of the temple is located?"

The priest smiled and motioned for Hilprecht to follow. He led the way down a dark hall to the far end of the structure and into a small room containing a heavy wooden chest which contained a few scraps of agate. Then the priest turned to Hilprecht and said:

"The two fragments of agate which you have listed as separate articles really belong together, for they are part of an inscribed votive cylinder of agate sent by King Kurigalzu to the temple. When the priests were ordered to make a pair of earrings for the statue of the god Ninib, we had no other agate except the cylinder, so it was cut into three parts, in this very room, each part bearing a portion of the inscription. One of those parts has been destroyed forever."

"Can you give me the original inscription?" asked Dr. Hilprecht.

Without hesitation, the phantom priest turned and with his finger wrote on the dust-covered wall in ancient Sumerian script: "To the god Ninib, son of Bel, his lord, has Kurigalzu, pontifex of Bel, presented this."

Suddenly Dr. Hilprecht seemed to be back in his library in Philadelphia with the white-robed priest still standing beside him. On a paper on the doctor's desk was the single word "Nebuchadnezzar" which two famous Egyptologists had translated to mean "Nebo, protect my work as a mason." The priest pointed to the word and said: "No, it means 'Nebo protect my boundary.'" An instant later he was gone.

The priest in Dr. Hilprecht's astounding dream had revealed the true location of the missing treasure room. He had correctly identified the two agate fragments as part of a single cylinder instead of separate objects, a fact later confirmed by modern Egyptologists, and he had corrected the translation of the word "Nebuchadnezzar" into the form now universally accepted by modern scholars.

But the phantom priest failed to explain the greatest mystery of all—how he solved these riddles after thirty centuries by Dr. Hilprecht's dream.

12

Unusual Dreams

There are a long list of cases where dreams seemed to project the dreamer into the past. But there are other cases where dreams also seem to project into the future, as in the case of a boy named Adrian Christian, who lived on the Isle of Man.

In the year 1833 he first dreamed that he was Captain of a ship. His brother, Thomas, was on another ship that was sinking and he rescued him. Adrian Christian told the story to his family, and his mother wrote it into the flyleaf of the family Bible, after Adrian Christian had exactly the same dream five times in the ensuing three years.

Forty-seven years later, in September of 1880, he had good reason to remember that dream. He was the Captain of the ship, British India, out of Sydney bound for Rangoon. While taking a nap one afternoon, he dreamed once again that his brother was on a ship that was sinking. That night he had the same dream again, except that he saw the word "family" scrawled on a piece of paper.

Captain Christian ordered the course of his own vessel altered to due north, which took them into some dangerous waters. Next day, September 6, 1880, he sighted a sinking vessel and rescued 269 persons, including his brother, Thomas, who was the skipper of the sinking vessel, a ship named The Family!

There is also the well-documented case of James Watt, inventor of the steam engine. In Watt's day the manufacture of ordinary lead shot for fowling pieces was an awkward process which involved drawing the lead into wire and chopping the wire into bits, or of chopping sheet lead into small squares and rolling the squares under heavy iron plates until they became roughly ball-shaped. Neither process was satisfactory and neither was cheap.

Then James Watt had a strange dream. According to his own story, he had the same dream night after night for almost a week. In it he seemed to be walking through a heavy rainstorm in which the rain itself turned to tiny leaden pellets which bounced about underfoot.

Was it significant? Did it mean that molten lead falling through the air would harden into tiny spherical pellets?

Unable to restrain his curiosity, Watt melted some lead over a small fire in a church steeple. He tossed a kettle full of the molten metal over the railing and watched it shower into a water-filled moat far below. When he searched the moat, he found that the lead had formed into round particles ideal for loading the guns.

As a result of this experiment, all other methods were discarded and from that day to this lead shot has been made by dropping molten metal into water—thanks to James Watt and his recurring dream.

For many years the pastor of the Rosedale Methodist Church in Winnipeg, Canada, was the Reverend Charles Morgan. It was customary for the musical director of the church to make a list of the hymns for the evening services and to give the list to Reverend Morgan who would then post them on the bulletin board.

The pastor had posted the list, as usual, and retired to his study for a short nap before the evening services began. He dreamed of the number of an old hymn which he had not heard in years. Then he dreamed of it again and in the background he heard a tumult of voices and the sound of rushing waters.

It was a disturbing dream. He'd felt as though he had been present at some great excitement which he could not see but could only hear the commotion and the insistent demand for that almost-forgotten hymn.

After the regular services had been concluded that evening, Reverend Morgan felt an overpowering compulsion to accede to the demands of the strange dream, and he asked the congregation to sing the hymn, the verse of which says:

"Hear, Father, while we pray to Thee for those in peril on the sea."

The date was April 14, 1912.

At the very moment Reverend Morgan's Winnipeg congregation was singing that hymn, one of the great sea tragedies of all time was taking place in the North Atlantic —the sinking of the Titanic.

From time immemorial men have been baffled, and ofttimes amazed, by the mental phenomena called dreams. Sometimes frightening, sometimes confusing, sometimes amusing—dreams occasionally have still another quality— that of seeming to transcend both time and space.

In a Baltimore grade school a seven-year-old boy offered the classic definition of dreams when he replied to his teacher: "Dreams are television that you see in your sleep."

In childish simplicity he had reduced the phenomena to understandable proportions. For dreams, like television, seem to enable the recipient to ignore time and distance with results which sometimes surpass the concepts of conventional science.

13

A Dream That Shook
The World

It was Sunday night in Boston, where Byron Somes was sleeping off a binge in his office at the Boston Globe.

It was Monday morning in the Straits of Sunda, where the mightiest explosion in the history of man had just taken place.

In his dream, Byron Somes had seen the catastrophe as clearly as though he had been watching it from mid-air, although he was actually twelve thousand miles away!

Two days before the Boston newsman's remarkable experience, nature had set the stage for catastrophe. The volcano of Krakatoa jutted up from an island in the Straits of Sunda, where an earthquake had torn the islands of Java and Sumatra apart in the year 1115. Krakatoa was noted for its rumblings and recurrent eruptions. On August 25th, 1883, it began deep underground mutterings which quickly reached the intensity of cannonading. By nightfall the volcano was showering the island with boulders. Bridges fell. Roads became impassable. Ships had to scurry out to sea to elude the stones. Great undersea explosions churned the seas around the island and the temperature of the water rose sixty-five degrees overnight.

By noon on the 26th, the great volcano Maha-Meru, Java's largest, had joined the thunderous chorus. Then Gunungguntur, and a few hours later the entire volcanic chain of the Kadangs was trumpeting its fury. The howitzers of Hell were in full volume. The sea boiled around the doomed island. The earth trembled. The nights were ruddy with the glow from the seething volcanoes—fifteen of them roaring in unison.

Suddenly there was one explosion so vast that it defies description—the island of Krakatoa had disintegrated in one cataclysmic blast that sent earthshocks and air waves around the globe. The tidal waves killed tens of thousands of persons, some of them hundreds of miles from Krakatoa. There has been nothing like it in the annals of the human race.

In Boston, on that hot Sunday night in August of 1883, Byron Somes awakened from his troubled sleep and sat there for a while pondering the nightmare he had just experienced. He could still hear in his mind the screams of those doomed mortals on that little tropical island as they sought vainly to escape from the fiery fate that engulfed them.

Somes jotted down the details of the dream while they were fresh in his mind, on the off chance that it might be usable as feature material some dull newsday. He marked the notes as 'important'—put them on his desk and went home.

There was little news of the great Krakatoa disaster next day, for communications to the stricken sector were sparse at best and the blast had virtually erased them.

A Dream That Shook The World

Somes did not report for work that day but someone evidently found his notes and misinterpreted them as a report on the seismological disturbance that was puzzling the experts. Something tremendous had happened—but where? Then came a fragmentary report from Batavia that located the disaster at Krakatoa—and the Boston Globe, on August 29th, ran an excellent story based on the details in the notes Somes had jotted down. Other papers evidently predicated their stories on that of the Boston Globe—and in a matter of a short time his remarkable dream had been translated into widespread newspaper copy.

When his employers found Somes and demanded details and more copy, Somes broke down and admitted that his 'report' was not intended as news matter—that it was nothing more than notes on a nightmare.

The higher-ups at the Globe probably experienced a nightmare of sorts at the discovery that they had printed a dream as though it were factual news—and had permitted other papers to duplicate it. Byron Somes was in the doghouse—and out of the newspaper business.

Before the Globe could make public confession, nature rescued them. Great waves began hammering at the west coast of the United States, seismic waves generated by the explosion of Krakatoa thousands of miles away. News of the disaster began filtering in as survivors reached cities where telegraph facilities still functioned.

As the newswires brought in the real story, hour by hour, the amazing accuracy of the account based on the dream of Byron Somes became evident. That bewildered fellow found himself in the good graces of the Globe again. And the paper declined, at the time, to reveal the story behind the story. [Eventually, the Globe 'explained' that

Somes's account of the Krakatoa disaster had been based on information from a coffee broker; later this was amplified to include another 'explanation' that Somes had also been doing some research on volcanoes in tropical islands at the time of the Krakatoa incident, etc. Author's Note]

In his remarkable dream Byron Somes, in Boston, seems to have witnessed the explosion of Krakatoa, halfway 'round the world, at approximately the time it happened. His dream was translated (accidentally perhaps) into a news story which was subsequently confirmed by conventional processes.

During the dream Somes kept hearing the word 'Pralape.' It made no sense at the time, but years later, through a Dutch historical society, he learned that Pralape was an ancient native name for Krakatoa, unused for nearly two centuries before he heard it in his "dream that shook the world."

14

The Double Mystery of Edwin Drood

Mystery stories were relatively new when Wilkie Collins induced his friend, Charles Dickens, to turn his talents in that direction. Dickens considered it carefully for several months before he began the writing of his first, and only, novel of that type—"The Mystery of Edwin Drood."

He had made arrangements to have the story published in twelve monthly installments in a magazine; and, oddly enough, for the first time in his career Dickens had insisted that the contract provide for payment to his heirs in case of his death.

If that provision was based on premonition, it was certainly well-founded, for Dickens died in 1870, when he had completed only six installments of his intriguing mystery story. Readers on both sides of the Atlantic were left to speculate on the solution which Dickens had in mind—a secret that had died with him, since he left no notes which might have provided a clue.

But the answer to their questions was on its way, through (or *from*) a young tramp printer who strolled into Brattleboro, Vermont, in the year following Dickens' death. Thomas P. James was an easy going, handsome, irresponsible girl-chaser in addition to being an excellent printer. Spotting a very pretty young lady, James followed her home and rented a room just across the street from the young girl's residence.

He soon discovered that he was rooming at the home of an elderly lady who was an advocate of spiritualism, then very much in vogue. For about a year he attended occasional sittings in his landlady's parlor, at which the customary trances and rappings occurred.

If James was inspired or affected in any way, he kept it to himself—until October 3, 1872, when he informed his landlady that he had been in contact with the spirit of Charles Dickens and the eminent author had given him power of attorney to complete the unfinished novel "The Mystery of Edwin Drood."

The good landlady was flabbergasted to think that her carefree young boarder was so highly regarded by the late, great Mr. Dickens. Eager to do her bit, she gave James free board and lodging until he completed the task.

Numerous witnesses later testified that James would retire to his room, slump into a chair and go into trances that often lasted for hours. Afterward, young James would write furiously, explaining to his friends that he was creating nothing . . . merely writing down the material which Dickens had given to him while he was entranced.

Sometimes the material covered many pages; at other times it consisted of only a few lines. Spirits, it seemed, had difficulties in transmission when the weather was bad. And when the young tramp printer had his mind on some pretty girl (as he frequently did) the eminent Mr. Dickens had to wait . . . wherever he was.

Word of the strange project leaked out, of course, and

newspapers promptly smelled a hoax. They set up a hue and cry of fraud, a sort of backfire which they felt would foredoom this young charlatan's work to failure.

They reckoned without their manuscript, for when it appeared in the bookstalls on October 31, 1873, less than a year after James began his task, even the experts of the literary world had to admit they were astounded. Here was a work by an unknown which sounded exactly as though Dickens himself had written it—or, as James asserted —had dictated it.

The obscure young tramp printer became a literary lion almost overnight. A paper in Springfield, Massachusetts, called him—"a worthy successor to Dickens himself!" A Boston paper said—"James could not have written this book without help from Dickens—be it spiritual or otherwise we do not know."

It remained for Sir Arthur Conan Doyle, the ingenious creator of the immortal Sherlock Holmes, to investigate the strange case of Thomas James. In the December, 1927, issue of the Fortnightly Review, Doyle reports that James showed no literary talent whatever, either before or after that one manuscript. His education had ended at the age of thirteen when he had completed a course comparable to the fifth grade in the average public school. Yet, somehow James had acquired the style and vocabulary and thinking processes of the great Charles Dickens—inexplicable accomplishments for a poorly educated employee of an American printing shop.

Sir Arthur Doyle concludes: "If it be indeed a parody it has the rare merit among parodies of never accentuating or exaggerating the peculiarities of the original."

And what of the young printer, Thomas James? He

dropped from sight as quickly as he had risen, and died in complete obscurity. In a few libraries there remain copies of what is called the James version of The Mystery of Edwin Drood . . . a mystery within a mystery.

15

The Man From Nowhere

He was a strange one all right . . . just as the authorities said . . . this young man who acted as though he had just dropped in from another world. . . .

He was just outside the new gate entrance to the city of Nuremberg, Germany, when an inquisitive policeman first noticed him. He was clean, but so poorly dressed that he was almost ragged. The policeman later told his superiors that he had first been attracted to the young man by the difficulty with which he seemed to walk . . . as though suffering from some deformity which caused him to stumble. His feet were badly swollen; his eyes were squinted against the light. . . .

The inquisitive policeman tried to question the lad but he learned nothing . . . over and over the stranger kept repeating. . . .

"I want to be a soldier like my father was!"

It did not sound like an expression of determination . . . but more like a chant . . . as though the strange young man who uttered it was merely reciting words he did not understand.

The policeman led him to the station, where the Mayor

and other local dignitaries gathered to observe and question this unusual visitor. In a monotone the young man continued to repeat his assertion that he wished to be a soldier like his father.

His name? He evidently did not understand what they were saying and he stared blankly. But when a pen was placed in his hand he giggled nervously and wrote in a slow, legible hand . . . K A S P E R   H A U S E R. He could not . . . or would not . . . write anything else. But on that quiet Whitmonday afternoon in 1828, the young man had inscribed on the records the name that was to mark the beginning of a puzzle which remains unsolved to this day.

When food was placed before him, he seized it in his hands and crammed it into his mouth as though he were famished. A mug of cold milk was evidently something he had never encountered before and he recoiled from it. Water he drank, but not until he had sampled it with a forefinger.

Just before nightfall, while the baffled city fathers of Nuremberg were trying to decide what to do with their enigmatic visitor, he presented them with two more pieces to the puzzle . . . two letters wrapped in rags which he carried inside his tattered vest. One letter purported to be from his mother. Dated sixteen years before, it urged anyone who found the boy to send him to Nuremberg when he was seventeen so he could enlist in the Sixth Cavalry of which his father had been a member, according to the letter.

The other missive was badly written and purported to be from someone who had found the boy and cared for him but who could no longer support him.

Oddly, both letters were written on some sort of thin

leather or parchment which was not familiar to the officials at Nuremberg.

Kasper Hauser, if that was indeed his name, spent that first night with the city's most learned man, Dr. Daumer, where the young man promptly astonished his host by trying to pick the flame off a candle. Further tests brought out that he had no depth perception whatever and, although he seemed to be in full possession of his faculties, they were as undeveloped as those of a baby.

Although the condition of his feet and legs indicated that he had walked a considerable distance, no one could be found who had seen him on the road. A reward was offered for anyone who could identify him. Pictures were distributed throughout Europe, but to no avail. The more the officials probed, the deeper the mystery of Kasper Hauser became.

Under the kind and patient tutelage of Dr. Daumer, Kasper Hauser learned quickly . . . first to speak . . . and then to write. He told his new-found friends that he had been raised since infancy in total darkness in a cellar . . . had never tasted anything except black bread and water . . . had never seen the man who brought his food in total darkness. He had seldom heard speech . . . and then only a few words. But how, or why, or where he had spent those years he had no idea.

In October of 1829, Kasper came stumbling out of Dr. Daumer's basement, bleeding from a deep gash on the head which he said had been inflicted by a masked man wielding a long knife. The city officials assigned two policemen to guard him after that . . . but while they dozed on the afternoon of December 14, 1833, Kasper Hauser went for a stroll in the park across the street . . . a stroll from which he came staggering back a few minutes later . . . dying from a stab wound which surgeons said could not have been self-inflicted.

The snow in the park revealed no footprints other than Kasper's . . . and no trace of the weapon.

The well-documented facts in the enigma of Kasper Hauser entitle it to a place in the records as one of the strangest cases of its kind.

Von Feurbach wrote of him . . . "Kasper Hauser showed such ignorance of the simplest facts of life . . . and such horror of the necessities of civilization . . . that one feels driven to believe that he was a native of another planet . . . transferred by some miracle to our own."

16

The Restless Dead

Scientists who investigated carefully and at length had to admit defeat; for they could arrive at no logical explanation for the strange events that were uncovered on the blazing afternoon of August 24, 1943, when a group of Masonic officials opened a sealed grave on the island of Barbados.

It was the tomb of Sir Evan McGregor, who had been buried there in 1841. But the Masons were not interested in Sir Evan — instead they wished to pay tribute to one Alexander Irvine — the father of Freemasonry in Barbados. Irvine's remains had been placed in the same vault, prior to McGregor.

The crypt itself had been carved out of the native stone of the island, and was so constructed that it projected about four feet above ground, resting on a concrete and brick base which extended underground to a depth of four feet. Entrance could be obtained only by descending a flight of six steps and opening a sealed door. After the heavy cover slab had been removed, it was found that the doorway to the vault itself was sealed by being bricked up.

As the bricks were being removed, while the waiting Masonic officials sweltered, the workmen called attention to a metal object of some sort that was visible through the aperture where the bricks were being taken out.

A little more careful work and the nature of the metal object became unmistakable — it was a coffin sheathed in lead, leaning against the only door to the crypt, head downward. Little by little the bricks were removed and the heavy coffin eased away from the door until it rested once again on the floor.

The Masonic delegation was understandably mystified. How did this 600-pound lead coffin of Sir Evan McGregor get out of its niche on the opposite side of the vault? What could have moved it after the vault had been carefully sealed more than a century before? And what had caused the three tiny holes in the lead where it had been sealed with solder?

Confused though they were, the Masons had little time to ponder the problems presented by this state of affairs, for they had another puzzle on their hands. There was no trace of either the coffin or the body of Alexander Irvine! His remains had vanished completely from the niche in the vault where they had rested when McGregor's coffin had been placed beside them. Both men had been entombed in heavy lead-covered coffins, placed side by side on cement shelves. Now, one coffin had vanished; and the other had somehow managed to cross the crypt and end up in a standing position against the sealed door.

The Masons placed a guard at the tomb and went away to ponder the puzzle. They reported to the authorities of Barbados, who in turn promptly called in several learned men to conduct an investigation. Examination of the records showed that both men *had* been entombed in that same crypt and the crypt sealed.

All witnesses agreed that the seals had not been broken and that the crypt had been in perfect condition when the workmen began to open it on that hot afternoon of August 24, 1943. Yet, somehow and sometime, very strange things had happened inside the vault.

After lengthy deliberation and careful investigation the scientists came away as baffled as the Masons had been. All of them went away to ponder the unexplained disappearance of Alexander Irvine, whose remains should have been in the sealed tomb where they had been placed — except that they were not there — and nobody knows why.

The disturbances in the vault we have just mentioned are by no means unparalleled. Also on Barbados, but in a different cemetery, miles from the scene of the Irvine mystery, officials were plagued with the eerie antics of the coffins in the vault of the Chase family.

Time after time, as various members of the family were taken to the crypt for entombment, the other coffins inside the sealed tomb were found in wild disarray. In each case they found the heavy capstone in position, sealed with a thick layer of molten lead and no trace of tampering. And in each case when they finally removed the seals from the inner door they found the inside a shambles . . . coffins tumbled about.

The lead-covered box that contained the body of Thomas Chase was so heavy that it required eight good men to lift it, but time after time it was found upside down on the side of the crypt opposite the shelf on which it belonged. Oddly, and perhaps significantly, only two coffins remained untouched: Those of Mrs. Goddard, the original occupant of the tomb, and of a baby girl, Mrs. Goddard's granddaughter. Armed guards placed beside the vault day and night were unable to prevent recurrences of the disorder inside it . . . eventually the Chase family had to remove the bodies and re-entomb them elsewhere.

In the old Christ Church cemetery of Barbados, the Chase vault still stands, its heavy stones and coral intact and (appropriately enough) carved into the thick capstone is a large question mark — a reminder of the restless dead.

17

Icebergs In The Sky

Scientists have not yet found the answers to the great chunks of ice that come hurtling to earth, year after year. Where do they come from . . . and why?

The inhospitable moor which stretches alongside the Bristol Channel, in north Devon and Somerset, is noted chiefly for its fine sheep and the sought-after woolens woven from their fleece. But on the night of November 10, 1950, something new was added to the records of that quiet windswept countryside.

Several times during that particular night Edward Latham heard his sheep dog barking furiously. The collie did that only when something was amiss. Latham got up and went outside. The sky was clear, the weather chilly, but not colder than the wind which romped over the moor and probed through his garments. Seeing nothing unusual, Latham decided that the dog was merely serving notice that it was on duty.

But when morning came, Latham had a surprise awaiting him. His dog was again barking furiously; this time in the field about fifty yards from the house. When Latham reached the spot, he found one of his sheep lying dead, a deep diagonal slash across the shoulders and down the neck, as though it had been struck with an axe. Beside the body of the sheep was a chunk of ice which he later ascertained weighed fourteen pounds . . . a chunk of ice that had fallen with such velocity that it was buried into the sod to a depth of about eight inches.

Latham later told authorities, "That sheep had been killed as if it had been struck by lightning! Around the field and down the roadway I found many other chunks of clear, hard ice, most of them the size of dinner plates or larger. I had never seen its equal!"

After lengthy investigation, the British Air Ministry had to admit it was baffled. The ice had not come from planes or from storms, and strangely enough the Air Ministry added, "The conditions do not suggest that this is any normal meteorological or weather phenomenon. . . ."

The excitement over this incident had hardly subsided before it was repeated, on November 24, 1950. Again the weather was mild, the skies were clear. During the early hours of the night, a chunk of ice, a one foot cube of it, came plunging to earth. It crashed through the roof of a garage in Wandsworth, near London, and made such a bang that the nightwatchman called police and reported a bomb explosion. Again, scientific study by the Air Ministry failed to solve the riddle.

These unexplained ice falls were by no means peculiar to England. In the middle of April, 1958, a shower of ice came rattling down into the yard of Mr. and Mrs. Leo Kozlowski in Napa, California; big, jagged pieces of ice that were from two to twelve inches in diameter. Some of them buried half their length in the earth. No planes were in the area. . . .

And then there was the remarkable experience of Edwin Groff, a farmer near Reading, Pennsylvania. He heard a whistling sound and a moment later a fifty pound chunk of ice about two feet in diameter smacked into the earth only a short distance from where he stood. He called his wife, and as they stood looking at the first chunk of ice, another, slightly smaller, came whistling down.

They called the sheriff . . . he called the Air Force . . . they called a meteorologist, and he called it natural ice that had been carried on the jet stream . . . that great river of air that wraps itself around the globe from west to east at speeds up to three hundred miles an hour, but the jet stream theory of the falling ice had to be abandoned for the simple reason that it could not carry chunks of ice suspended in mid-air.

Ed Groff's ice blocks came whistling down on July 30, 1957. On August 14, more ice came down in formidable chunks at Gowen City, Pennsylvania . . . and on September 8, 1958, a whopping big chunk of ice roared through the roof of a warehouse at 510 North Third Street in Chester, Pennsylvania. Like the others, it defied any explanation which covered the facts.

Strangest of all, perhaps, was the experience which befell Mr. and Mrs. Dominic Bacigalupo of 336 Greystone Road, Old Bridge, New Jersey, on the night of September 2, 1958. They were watching television in their living room about 9:00 p.m. when Mr. Bacigalupo went to the kitchen to get himself some coffee. As he sat down in front of the TV set, there was a shattering roar . . . a chunk of ice had torn a three-foot hole in the roof and through the ceiling of the kitchen.

Like all the similar falls before it, it remains unexplained.

As the British Air Ministry said, "This phenomenon is one of the biggest mysteries of the century. . . ."

18

The Flatwoods Monster

Those who saw the thing were terrified. Those who investigated were convinced that it had been there. But what it was and where it came from constitute the mystery of the Flatwoods monster.

It was just getting dark on that warm September evening in 1952 when the five youngsters stopped their play to watch the strange spectacle overhead. Outlined against the sky over the nearby mountains was a disc-shaped object which was spurting little streams of sparks. It wobbled a bit, moved on hesitantly and dropped slowly down toward the mountaintop, where it settled among the trees.

Whatever it was, it did not resemble any plane the youngsters had ever seen. They realized that this was some sort of emergency and they scattered to their respective homes to report. Eddie May, 13, and his brother Fred, 12, ran to the nearby house where their mother operated a beauty parlor in the little West Virginia community of 300 population.

The boys told their mother excitedly that they and their companions had seen a plane or a flying saucer land on the foothill that towered above the town.

Mrs. May was skeptical, of course, but the skepticism disappeared when she stepped outside to see for herself. There, dimly visible several hundred yards away near the top of the hill, was a slowly pulsating red light. Something was on the ground there, just as the children said . . . but what was it? Mrs. May sent the boys running to the nearby home of Gene Lemon, 17, a member of the National Guard.

Armed only with a flashlight, Lemon led the party up the hill. In addition to Mrs. May and her two sons, the group also included 14-year-old Neil Nunley, and a pair of ten-year-olds who had also seen the object land, Ronnie Shaver and Tommy Hyer.

The experience they encountered in the ensuing minutes put the little community of Flatwoods on the front pages of the world's newspapers.

Lemon and the Nunley boy were about fifty feet ahead of the rest of the party as they hurried up the brush-covered hillside.

They noticed a light mist which drifted before them and as they got closer they detected a pungent, irritating odor about it. Near the top of the hill, where the unpleasant odor was strongest, they spotted a glowing red object which pulsated slowly . . . like a faintly glowing mass of red coals, they said. For the moment they forgot about the irritating aroma that swirled about them. Lemon and Nunley reached an old gateway from which they could see the red object clearly . . . a thing about 25 feet in diameter and perhaps six feet high. . . . Should they approach it? As they paused, Mrs. May and the other boys joined them.

The attention of the entire group was directed to this strange glowing thing on the ground about seventy-five feet away and, for a moment, none of the group noticed the

79

other object, hardly twenty feet away, among the bushes to their right.

The dog that had accompanied the party growled and bristled and the entire group turned to see what was wrong. Gene Lemon flashed his light among the bushes. Mrs. May screamed.

Whatever it was, it was alive . . . and it was a giant by human standards. The flashlight showed the head and shoulders of a creature slightly less than ten feet tall. It appeared to be wearing a helmet of some sort, projecting from a dark blue-green or greenish-gray body which reflected the flashlight beams like rubberized silk.

The most awesome part of the scene was the thing's face . . . almost round and blood red . . . with two greenish-orange eyes which glowed in the flashlight beams as do the eyes of certain fish and some wild animals. But this was neither fish nor wild animal.

The thing moved. Its lower extremities were concealed by the brush and weeds . . . but all agreed that it didn't walk . . . it seemed to slide its feet, if it had any. There was a hissing sound, and a powerful sickening odor pervaded the scene.

Lemon's dog fled. Lemon dropped his flashlight. The entire party of seven panicked and raced pell-mell down the hillside. Once safely away from the scene of their terrifying experience they phoned the Sheriff at nearby Sutton, West Virginia. He and a deputy were miles away on another call to check on a report that a plane had crashed . . . possibly the same object that had been seen at Flatwoods. Someone notified Lee Stewart, Jr., editor of the Braxton newspaper. . . . He reached Flatwood about thirty minutes after the incident had occurred and found Mrs.

May hysterical . . . the boys in a state of shock.

Finally Gene Lemon led another armed party back to the hilltop. The strange, sickening odor was still there . . . but the monster and the huge pulsating red object were gone.

Not without a trace, however, for, in the soil where the horrible thing had stood, the searching party found unexplained skid marks . . . which may have been the only earthly trace of the Flatwoods monster.

19

Sky Traps

In a comparatively small area off the southeast coast of the United States, more than a score of modern planes have vanished without a trace, carrying crews and passengers to oblivion. The mysterious loss of all these lives in this one area has earned for it the ominous title— Point of No Return.

Let's look at the record.

At ten-thirty on the night of January 29, 1948, the big British four-engined airliner, Star Tiger, radioed that she was on course, four hundred miles from Bermuda enroute to Kingston, twenty-six passengers and crew members aboard. Good weather and no trouble.

That was the last ever heard from her. Not another radio message of any kind, not a single trace of wreckage, not even an oil slick to mark a watery grave. The Star Tiger was gone.

At 7:45 on the morning of January 17, 1949, Captain J C. McPhee lifted the Ariel off the runway at Bermuda for a trip to Kingston, Jamaica, a thousand miles away. The Ariel, a sister ship to the ill-fated Star Tiger, was carrying fuel for an extra ten hours of flight, just in case. Forty minutes after it left Bermuda, Captain McPhee radioed that he had reached cruising altitude, wind and weather fair, expected arrival at Jamaica on time.

After that, only silence. Intensive search failed to produce a single scrap of evidence which might indicate what had happened. Like the Star Tiger before her, the Ariel had met her fate so abruptly that there had been no time to radio for help.

The Star Tiger and the Ariel had followed the pattern of another tragedy of the same type which had occurred on December 5, 1945.

As part of the routine pilot training at the Naval Air Station in Fort Lauderdale, Florida, the planes take off for short, triangular trips over the nearby ocean. The planes fly a pre-determined plan which takes them eastward a given distance, then they make a sharp turn to cover the second leg of the course, and finally another sharp-angled turn and back to base. On the afternoon of December 5, 1945, five TBM Avenger propeller-driven torpedo bombers left the base for one of these routine flights—160 miles eastward—40 miles north—then southwest back to base. They had done it many times before and there was no reason to believe that this trip would be different.

One of the planes on that flight carried two men; the others carried three each. All the planes were equipped with the best radio and navigational equipment; all the crew members were experienced and competent.

At two minutes past two o'clock, according to the official records of that fateful afternoon, the first plane took to the air. Six minutes later all five were in flight, cruising in formation and still climbing as they swung lazily eastward over the rim of the Atlantic at slightly more than 200 miles per hour.

At three-forty-five came the first inkling of trouble. By that time the planes should have been asking for landing instructions—instead—the base radio got an urgent message from the flight commander. . . . "Can't see land. . . . Can't be sure where we are. . . . We are not sure of our position—." All five of the navigators lost at the same time? There was something incredible about that!

The misgivings at the base were well founded . . . for fifteen minutes later the tower heard the planes talking anxiously among themselves . . . and to their astonishment heard the flight commander turn control over to another flier. At four-twenty-five the last message from the doomed flight came in . . . "not certain where we are . . . about 225 miles northeast of base. —Looks like we are—" The voice broke off . . . and after that, only silence.

Emergency measures were quickly instituted. A Martin flying boat with crew of thirteen and full rescue equipment roared out from the base . . . only to vanish five minutes later without a trace. Coast Guard planes scoured the ocean in that area all night. At daybreak the big aircraft carrier, Solomons, was on the scene, adding her scores of planes to the search work. Altogether 21 vessels were there by nightfall, along with more than 300 planes and twelve land parties which were searching the beaches. Net result—nothing. Not a single trace of man or machine. Not a scrap of clothing, nor an oil slick. And there has been none to this day.

The Naval Board of Inquiry which probed the case knew that the Avengers should, under any conceivable circumstances, have radioed an alarm. Some of the crewmen could have escaped by parachute.

Debris should have been found had they fallen into

the sea. Instead there was nothing. And the Martin flying boat could land on the sea, had emergency radio sending equipment—but it, too, vanished into the void without a trace, less than five minutes after it left the base.

The fate of the five Avengers and their crews and of the flying boat which disappeared in search of them, remains another unsolved mystery. After a lengthy investigation the Naval Board report says:

"—We are not able to even make a good guess as to what happened."

20

A Handful
of Murder

If the officers from Scotland Yard thought they were engaged in another routine murder case, they could hardly have been farther from the truth.

The old man whose body was sprawled in front of the fireplace was dead, no doubt about that. The room, like the body, was quite cold. It was apparent to the boys from Scotland Yard that the victim had been done in by liberal applications of the andirons. On the question of who had used the weapons, however, they were completely in the dark.

Robbery could not be ruled out as a possible motive, though there was little in the shabby elegance of the quarters to indicate any wealth worthy of the name. The suddenly-deceased was not known to be a quarrelsome man and he had no known enemies.

Scotland Yard was stumped.

As the detectives were bundling up their cameras and measuring tapes and preparing to leave, an impeccably attired young man appeared at the door. Could he be of service? Well, in such cases you don't overlook anything, not even a fop, so detectives led the young man into the room where the deed had been done. He glanced around casually and asked if he might examine one of the numerous bloody handprints which marked the walls.

Head cushioned in the palm of his hand, he gazed steadfastly at one of the gruesome prints, then he turned to police and said:

"The murderer is a young man, gentlemen. Furthermore, he is well-to-do, he carries a small gold watch in his left front trouser pocket . . . and he is a near relative of the old gentleman whose body was just taken from this room."

The angry Scotland Yard boys were ready to toss this smug dandy out on his ear for wasting their time, but there were a couple of correspondents for the London papers on hand and they smelled a story. Who was this fancy dresser who presumed to deduce so much from a mere bloody handprint on a grimy wall?

Cheiro—Cheiro the Great! he told them as he handed them his lavishly embossed business card.

The story made the papers on the following day, and twenty-four hours later the extraordinary palmist was back in the headlines, for the police had found their man. The murderer was not only young and well-to-do, but he carried a gold watch in his left front trouser pocket, and he was the son of the murdered man . . . the near relative whom Cheiro had described so well.

In a matter of weeks Cheiro became the rage of London. Only a few close friends remembered him as Count Louis Hamon; his transformation into a sensational public figure bore little resemblance to the Count. He basked in the spotlight and banked substantial sums each week, the proceeds from his new career of counseling his wealthy clients on their futures.

Cheiro left England in 1893 for New York, where he

established himself in a lavish suite of offices on Park Avenue. Again success came easily for him; and, as clients streamed into his doors, it was inevitable that the newspapers should be close behind. A young lady from the New York World inquired whether he would be willing to submit to a series of public tests which the publisher of the paper had in mind. It was a crucial moment for Cheiro. If he declined the test he was ruined. If he accepted and failed to convince the skeptics, he would also be ruined. Yet, without a moment's hesitation he accepted the veiled threat of exposure.

The World publicized the test widely, using it as a circulation-building stunt. On the day of the test, Cheiro was the calmest person in the room. The test itself consisted of thirteen palm prints of thirteen different New York citizens. The papers which bore the palm prints bore no identifying marks of any kind. Only the three judges knew whose prints they were and the judges sat grim-faced and silent, waiting for Cheiro to blunder.

Without hesitation, he picked up print after print and after a cursory glance, accurately described the persons to whom the prints belonged. But when he reached the 13th and final print he hesitated. Dropping the print face down on the table he slowly turned to the judges and said:

"Gentlemen, I refuse to identify this print. . . ."

A ripple of excitement ran through the crowded room. Was he stumped?

Holding up his hand for silence, Cheiro went on— "I refuse to identify this print to anyone but the owner— because it is the mark of a murderer. He will give himself away through his self-confidence and will die in prison in great anguish."

88

Cheiro had been playing cat and mouse with the judges. He had scored one hundred percent on the test, for that last print had been that of Dr. Henry Meyer, caught when he bragged of his crime, adjudged guilty and insane. Dr. Meyer died in an institution for the criminally insane.

The newspapers were generous in their praise of Cheiro. His fame spread around the world. His triumphal tour of Europe was highlighted when he predicted in 1897 that Czar Nicholas would live unhappily only to lose everything, including his life (as he did) in 1917.

But Cheiro's remarkable talents deserted him in 1906 and he retired. Lawsuits plagued him, and a conviction on a charge of mishandling a client's money sent him to prison for 13 months. One morning in 1936, police found him lying on the sidewalks of Hollywood and he died on the way to the hospital, victim of a stroke.

Cheiro's claim that he never understood his strange talent may have been true, for in the final analysis he became another baffled has-been . . . a magician who seemed to have lost his magic.

21

Idiot Genius

Ignorant, dirty and ridiculed by those who knew him, the plowboy drew roars of laughter when he told the people that the king had need of his wisdom. But it was true . . . and history has no stranger story than that of the idiot genius, Robert Nixon.

His parents were pitifully poor farmers who worked in the fields from dawn to dark in order to eke out an existence. Robert Nixon was an only child, large-boned, dull-witted, and generally regarded in the area around Bridge House Farm, Cheshire, as more than a little stupid. His parents evidently shared that last opinion, for after only a few days' schooling, they gave up and sent him back to the plow.

That's where he was on that fateful day in 1485 when the fate of Britain hung in the balance at Bosworth Field. The legions of King Richard were locked in mortal combat with the army led by Henry, the Earl of Richmond, many miles from the field where dull-witted Robert Nixon trudged along behind the old horse, turning the soil with a crude wooden plow.

Suddenly, in mid-furrow, Nixon stopped. He stood head down for a moment, as though he were listening. Then he

90

began to hop about the plowed ground, waving his arms, stumbling, pointing, and yelling. The lad had done some strange things before, but nothing like this! The overseer hurried across the field to stop this nonsense and to get the boy back to work.

But he, too, stopped short, for Robert was clearly out of his mind; eyes staring, mouth foaming, arms waving, and he was yelling. Brandishing a whip he carried, he screamed. . . . "There Richard! . . . there! . . . now!" A moment later. . . . "Up, Henry! Up with all arms! Over the ditch, Henry . . . over the ditch and the battle is won!" He stood there for a few minutes as one transfixed, and then he began to smile. Taking notice of the overseer for the first time, the boy said. . . . "The battle is over . . . Henry has won!" Then he went back to his plowing as if nothing had happened.

The overseer hurried away to report to his masters, the Lords of Cholmondeley, for it had been noticed that stupid Robert Nixon had a knack of knowing things that were happening at a distance, and things that were going to happen. He had predicted a fire in the nearby village, and the death of a member of the Cholmondeley family. He had foretold a great storm two weeks in advance, and had predicted that Henry and Richard would fight at Bosworth Field. Now he was claiming that Richard was defeated . . . no longer King! Was it true or false? Two days later came messengers from the palace . . . King Henry VII had succeeded to the throne. But when the messengers reached the village of Over, where Nixon lived, they were puzzled to discover that the village had already known of Henry's ascension to the throne . . . thanks to Robert Nixon.

The King soon heard of Nixon . . . that strange youth

with that strange gift. The townspeople of Over were amused at Nixon's antics . . . for the boy ran through the village from house to house, begging people to hide him. The King's men were coming to take him to the palace, he screamed; and in the palace he would starve to death. That was a double-barreled joke! Imagine the King sending for such a dolt, and imagine anyone starving to death in the King's own palace!

Once again, Nixon had called the turn, for the King *did* send for him, paying his parents handsomely to turn over to him their much-maligned son. Just a few minutes before the King's messenger arrived, Nixon arose from the family table and said, "The King's man is coming soon. I must go but I will never return."

When the boy reached the palace, he found King Henry skeptical, doubly so when he saw what a dull-witted fellow he had sent for. Henry had hidden a ring, and he immediately demanded to know if Nixon could locate it. The boy gazed steadily at the King and said, "The ring is not lost, Sire, for he who hides can also find!"

Nixon's reply pleased the King, and he ordered that a scribe be kept at the boy's side day and night, to record any prophecies he might make. The records were made and studied, but not all of them had any meaning in the time of Henry VII . . . for some of the predictions ranged far in the future, to the great fire of London in 1666, and to the accession to the throne of the Four Georges from the House of Hanover. Old records show that the boy also predicted events which have yet to transpire—the invasion of Britain by soldiers with ice on their helmets; and, as he put it, "The bear that has been tied to the stake shall shake off his chains and cause much debate and strife."

King Henry ignored Nixon's pleas not to leave him in the castle when the King left on a hunting trip. Instead, the monarch named a special deputy to care for Nixon while the King was away. The deputy locked the boy in a room, went away on a trip himself, and forgot to leave instructions where the boy could be found. Upon the King's return, a search was instituted, and Nixon was found—another prediction fulfilled—for he had died of starvation in the King's palace.

22

Incredible Cremations

Fire was one of man's first friends. He learned to use it at the entrance to his caves to defend himself from his enemies. Later he tamed fire and forced it to help him do his work. But from time to time it still serves notice that man has not fully mastered it—that fire has secrets still withheld from him.

Sometimes these secrets are exhibited in the form of ghastly pranks that make headlines before they are filed away, unexplained.

On the morning of Monday, July 2, 1951, Mrs. P. M. Carpenter of 1200 Cherry Street, Northeast, in St. Petersburg, Florida, went to the door of the room occupied by Mrs. Mary H. Reeser, 67, whom she had last seen the night before. As the landlady approached Mrs. Reeser's door it was a few minutes past eight—time for their morning coffee—and she also wanted to deliver a telegram which the Western Union boy had been unable to deliver because Mrs. Reeser did not answer his knock.

That was odd, Mrs. Carpenter thought, for Mrs. Reeser was a light sleeper. Was something wrong?

Definitely, yes!

Mrs. Carpenter took hold of the doorknob to Mrs.

Reeser's room and jerked her hand away with a cry of pain. The brass doorknob was so hot it had burned her hand! . . . Frightened, she ran outside and called for help. Some house painters working nearby dropped their work and hurried to her. Together they forced the door to Mrs. Reeser's room, and walked into a gruesome mystery that has never been solved.

Although the windows were open, the apartment was unbearably hot. Near the front window were the charred remains of a big armchair, and the equally charred remains of Mrs. Reeser. There was little left of either.

Police were called. They in turn called in the fire department experts and then pathologists were brought to the scene of the mystery. Their intensive and prolonged investigation developed strange facts, some of which do not coincide with scientific understanding of fire.

It was ascertained that Mrs. Reeser had last been seen alive about nine o'clock on the preceding evening when her son, Dr. Richard Reeser, her landlady, Mrs. Carpenter, and another friend had told her goodnight as she sat in the big easy chair where she died. She had been wearing a rayon nightgown, cloth bedroom slippers, and a light housecoat.

When the painters and the landlady forced their way into her room on that fateful morning, Mrs. Reeser's one hundred and seventy pounds had been reduced to less than ten pounds of charred material by the same fierce heat which had destroyed the chair. Only her left foot, her shrunken skull, and a few vertebrae were unconsumed by the flames. Of the big chair, only the coil springs remained.

The room in which Mary Reeser died in this inferno showed little effects of the heat. The walls were covered with a sooty deposit from a point about four feet above the floor. The drapes were thickly coated. A mirror on the wall about ten feet from the chair had cracked from the intense heat. Twelve feet from the fire, two tall candles had melted and congealed in pink puddles on a dressing table, their wicks lying limply across the metal holders. The effects of the heat were numerous and plain above that four-foot mark, but below it the fire had left only two marks. Directly beneath the chair there was a small burned spot on the rug. Beside the chair a plastic electric wall outlet had melted, blowing a fuse which stopped the victim's electric clock at twenty minutes past four.

The authorities were baffled by the strange death of Mary Reeser.

Edward Davies, arson specialist for the National Board of Underwriters, made a thorough investigation and had to admit that he could only say that the victim had died from fire, with no idea what caused it.

Famed pathologist, Dr. Wilton Korgman of the University of Pennsylvania, fared no better His report said: "Never have I seen a skull so shrunken nor a body so completely consumed by heat. This is contrary to normal experience and I regard it as the most amazing thing I have ever seen."

Routine checks ruled out the possibility of lightning—there had been none in St. Petersburg that night. A cigarette, igniting her clothing? Experts pointed out that clothing could not have produced the 2500-degree heat which had been required for such drastic results. A short circuit? Again the answer was no, for the melting wall socket had blown the fuses after the fire had begun. Gasoline, perhaps? FBI pathologists checked; reported that there had been no fluids or chemicals to induce burning.

Unsolved, and apparently unsolvable, the strange case of Mary Reeser dropped from the headlines. Over the nation a few editors recalled similar cases and mentioned them briefly but by and large the matter was forgotten.

The bedeviled authorities of St. Petersburg felt constrained to make some official statement on which to close the bizarre incident. Months after the tragedy, the Chief of Police and the Chief of Detectives signed a statement attributing the fiery death of Mary Reeser to falling asleep with a cigarette in her hand, igniting her clothing.

That convenient hypothesis had already been ruled out by the experts, but it served to close the case, awkwardly but legally. If the experts were baffled, then there was no reason to expect the police officers to do any better.

The strange death of Mary Reeser is but one of many similar cases.

All of them are mystifying. None of them has ever been explained.

23

The Strongest Man
On Earth

Not all giants are strong, and not all strong men are giants. Feats of strength vary greatly from one outstanding individual to another, some approaching the incredible. But among all of them one stands out.

The fabled Goliath of the Bible was a giant who hailed from Gath. Standing six cubits and one span, his eleven feet towered over the battlefield and he inspired terror by size alone. Goliath amused himself by throwing huge stones into the ranks of the enemy, making it all the more fitting that he should fall victim to a stone thrown back at him by David.

Claudius Caesar brought to Rome a strapping fellow called Baggaras, a giant Arab who reportedly stood nine feet tall. Like Goliath, he delighted in feats of strength, but the details are so hazy that it is impossible to determine exactly what he did, so he gets honorable mention on the list of mighty men.

Most giants are not especially strong. Their elongated arm and leg bones give them remarkable height without giving them the commensurate muscular structure needed for feats of strength. O'Byrne, the famed Irish Giant whose eight-feet-three inch skeleton stands in the Royal College of Surgeons in London, was typical; he was healthy and tall, but he often had difficulty coping with physical tasks which were no problem for smaller men.

The man who held the title was the exception to the rule. Angus McAskill, born in Scotland in 1825 was one of a family of thirteen normal children. His parents brought him to Nova Scotia when he was about twelve years old, and he worked in his father's sawmill at Englishtown. He seemed strong for a youngster. Angus was about six feet four when he was sixteen years old; at seventeen, he stood six feet seven.

Two years later people were stopping to stare at him, for on his nineteenth birthday Angus McAskill was seven feet, nine inches tall, and as powerful as he appeared to be. When one of his father's horses gave out, Angus slipped into the harness and matched his strength with the other horse. A moderate drinker, he once walked into a tavern, picked up a one hundred-and-forty-gallon puncheon and drank from the bunghole. Doctors in New York who measured him there in 1845 reported that his chest measured seventy inches, his weight was four hundred and five pounds, and none of it was fat.

Angus was a church-going, peace-loving young giant who sought no trouble but could take care of himself if forced to do so. A two-hundred-and-fifty-pound heavyweight fighter from the docks of New York badgered Angus into a match by accusing the Nova Scotian giant of cowardice. Surrounded by a boatload of professional gamblers, the fighter came to Englishtown to teach the young giant a lesson in the ring. Angus's friends had to dig and scrape to find enough money to cover the wagers of the gamblers who accompanied the professional fighter. Nobody had ever seen

Angus fight, but those who knew him best had never seen him turn back from a test of strength, however dangerous, so they backed him to the hilt.

The mob was screaming with excitement as the two men climbed into the ring in the old barn where the fight was to take place. The antagonists stepped to the center of the ring and clasped hands. Suddenly the professional fighter screamed and fell to his knees. The fight was over. Angus had simply crushed the man's hand with his own mighty grip.

P. T. Barnum heard of this congenial giant who lifted plow-horses over fences for fun, and Barnum took Angus on tour for five years, billing him with Tom Thumb as the world's largest and smallest humans. At the conclusion of each act, Tom Thumb danced a jig on the palm of the giant's hand.

McAskill's fatal weakness was the fact that he could not resist a wager where his great strength was involved. To win a dollar he once waded into a New York street that was knee-deep in mud and unhitched the horses that were unable to move a heavily-laden dray. While the crowd cheered, Angus threw his weight against the harness and slowly dragged the conveyance out of the mire.

Another wager eventually resulted in his death.

The amount at stake was one thousand dollars, and to win it he had to lift a ship's anchor weighing twenty-two hundred pounds. Angus had lifted greater weights, but this one was awkward because of its shape. Little by little he got the massive anchor balanced in his grip. Veins standing out like cords, face livid, Angus slowly raised the device above his head.

He had won the bet—but the cost was excessive. In lowering the anchor, one of the flukes struck his shoulder, throwing him dangerously off balance. The giant managed to avoid being crushed, but the fluke bruised his shoulder muscles—and the career of Angus McAskill faded rapidly.

He had saved his money and he retired to his home in Nova Scotia where he died in 1863. In his prime, there was none to challenge his claim to the title of Strongest Man in the World.

24

Midnight At Noon

Time after time, history records instances where sudden darkness blanketed cities and nations in midday.

What happened—and why?

According to the complex calculations of astronomers, the earth is swinging along through space at the rate of about 18,000 miles an hour. And according to many of these same astronomers, space is by no means empty. Billions of tiny particles are swept up in the Earth's atmosphere each day as we speed through space. Those astronomers who speak of the emptiness of space are contradicted by other savants who speak of the great masses of dust and gases which are sometimes so dense they are opaque.

If there are large masses of opaque and semi-opaque materials drifting in space, then it is conceivable that the earth may slice through them from time to time, with unusual results for those on hand to witness the event.

A thin layer of cosmic dust, obstructing the sun at a low angle, would cause a sharp decrease in light, even at midday. There are instances on record where sudden darkness has fallen briefly on sunshiny days, at times when no eclipse was recorded.

On April 26, 1884, Preston, England was the scene of a dramatic darkness at midday. News reports indicate that the sky simply turned black, as though a great curtain had been pulled over it. Alarmed citizens fumbled their way around the streets, animals went to bed, and the devout turned to prayer. Then, as suddenly as it began, the darkness was dissipated and daylight returned. The occurrence was never explained, although there were the customary official guesses until the subject had been replaced in the public mind.

There was at Aitkin, Minnesota, April 2, 1889, a sudden and intense darkness during which sand streamed down from the blackness. It, too, went unexplained. London was blacked out suddenly in mid-morning on August 19, 1763. This was an intense, paralyzing blackness which seemed impervious to candles and lanterns. Astronomers admitted there was no eclipse.

Oshkosh, Wisconsin, had a daytime blackout of unknown origin on March 19, 1886, which began at three o'clock in the afternoon and in five minutes plunged the city into pitch darkness. It lasted not more than ten minutes, according to officials, the blot of darkness moving from west to east in a sky that was thickly covered with clouds.

After the badly shaken city had regained its daylight, it learned that cities to the west of it had undergone similar experiences. Something had caused a relatively small spot of intense darkness to move from coast to coast in three hours or less; either a solid body of unknown type between the earth and the sun, or as seems less likely in this instance, a small but dense band of cosmic debris that blotted out the light as we sped through or near it.

Memphis, Tennessee, was going about its affairs as usual at ten o'clock in the morning of December 2, 1904, when for no apparent reason the sun vanished and darkness fell.

The ensuing fifteen minutes were a time of terror for many. In some quarters of the city there was shouting and screaming and anguished prayer by those who feared that the end of the world had come.

For psychological reasons, perhaps, these infrequent but disturbing periods of unscheduled darkness in daytime are explained away variously as forest fire smoke, unusual cloud formations, or dust clouds from distant deserts.

There are occasions when such explanations are doubtless justified. There are other incidents when such explanations are debatable to say the least, and one such instance occurred in September of 1950, when a large part of the United States experienced a weird blue sun that appeared to be shining weakly through a heavy filter. The phenomenon was noted in the United States on September 24. On the twenty-sixth, Scotland and England found that the sun had turned blue-green for them. In Denmark the blue sun lasted only two hours, but that was long enough for lines of depositors to form at the banks, eager to draw out their savings in case the end of the world had come.

Again, the ever ready official explanations were promptly made available. The American public was told that the peculiar appearance of the sun was due to smoke from a vast forest fire in Alberta, Canada. The smoke, so it was explained, rose to high level and acted as a dense filter which screened the sunlight to its unnatural hue.

There was one serious flaw in that explanation; for at the same time the alleged smoke was said to be riding the winds eastward across the United States, it was also moving westward across the state of Washington and obscuring the sun. It is an odd wind indeed that blows smoke in two opposite directions at the same time!

104

PART
TWO

25

Millionaire Mystic

He amassed a fortune, built thousands of miles of railroads, and founded forty towns, but he never made a move without consulting what he called his "Unseen Friends."

Like many another couple, Mr. and Mrs. Arthur Stilwell began their married life with little except each other. His parents were poor but thrifty Indiana farmfolk and had little enough for themselves. Arthur Stilwell was too proud to permit his wife's parents to share their meagre resources with him. He struck out on his own, and his first job was that of driving a freight wagon. A few weeks later he advanced to clerk, and there he stuck. He had barely finished high school, he had no money, his prospects of becoming a millionaire were not bright.

But night after night he continued to hear voices. Sometimes they came in his sleep—sometimes when he was sitting by the table lamp trying to read. It was by no means a new experience for him, and no longer frightening; for Arthur Stilwell had been hearing these little voices since he was fifteen. He recorded in his diary that a voice had told him he would meet and marry a girl named Genevieve Wood within four years. At the time he didn't even know anyone

107

by that name; but the prediction proved correct, just as the little voice had told him. From that time forward, Arthur Stilwell never doubted the wisdom of the voices; but he never talked about them except to his wife, for fear that people would think him demented.

Over and over again, as he fidgeted at his clerk's desk, the voice urged him to go West and build railroads, which were then spreading their steel tentacles in every direction. Finally Arthur and Jennie Stilwell gave in. He quit his job, packed their scant belongings in a borrowed cart, and set out for Kansas City.

He got a job there in a bond house and a brokerage firm, keeping his eyes and ears open, heeding again and again the little voices which he says urged him to build a railroad.

Incredible as it seems, this forty-dollar-a-week clerk did build a railroad. Bankers knew him and trusted him; money was easy, Stilwell quietly bought the land, assembled the funds, and before the surprised New York financiers realized what was happening, he had his Kansas City Belt Line Railroad in full operation, right under their noses.

In the remarkable career of this most unusual character, there is no stranger incident than that of his plans to build a railroad to link the wheatfields of Kansas with the Gulf of Mexico. It was a perfectly logical development which older men had overlooked. Stilwell, a twenty-six-year-old financier who claimed to be guided by spirit voices, saw the opportunity and took the plunge.

Time after time, when grave problems faced him, he would retire to his office, pull the shades and ask for guidance from his strange unseen counsellors. All went well until the railroad was only fifty miles from Galveston. He wrote later that he asked for guidance and was told to stop

108

construction at once, otherwise his career would be blighted —for Galveston was doomed.

Stilwell was in a quandary, of course. His business associates could not be expected to believe his story of such unconventional guidance—yet he had to order the change of destinations, quickly.

Stilwell squared his jaw and faced the storm. His business associates demanded an explanation of this expensive and outrageous decision. The citizens of Galveston were furious. But Stilwell stuck to his guns and the Kansas City Southern Railroad went to the Gulf of Mexico at a desolate spot which was called Port Arthur in honor of Arthur Stilwell. When the hurricane smashed Galveston to pieces, Port Arthur's piers and railroad facilities were untouched, and they played a major part in the emergency work. His business associates who had condemned him so bitterly, now commended him for his good luck. Stilwell, now known as "Lucky" Stilwell, only smiled and said nothing. He and Jennie had decided that people simply would not believe, nor would they understand, the strange counsellors on whom his million dollar ventures depended.

How could he ever explain that he had known the name of his wife four years before he met her—or the infallible advice that had taken him from penniless clerk to millionaire railroad builder in seven years—or the source of the surprising decision to turn his railroad away from Galveston to terminate it in a saltwater swamp?

Altogether he built seven railroads and the Port Arthur ship canal. He founded forty cities and towns, two of which were named for him—Port Arthur, Texas, and Stilwell, Oklahoma. He amassed a sizeable fortune in the course of his amazing career; for everything he touched turned to

money, a state of affairs which he attributed to his strange
counsellors.

Arthur Stilwell was not a spiritualist. He writes that he
attended one seance and that it bored him.

During his busy lifetime he found time to write and
publish thirty books, nineteen of which were novels, including The Light That Never Failed, a longtime best
seller. In 1910 he wrote a book which predicted in detail
the coming of World War One.

In 1914 he wrote another remarkable book: "To All
the World Except Germany," in which he predicted the
defeat of Germany and her allies, the collapse of the Russian monarchy, the independence of Finland and Poland,
and the restoration of Palestine to the Jews. Stilwell died
in 1928. Two weeks later his beloved Jennie stepped out
a skyscraper window in Manhattan to join the husband
who had been chosen for her by his mysterious voices so
many years before.

26

The Case of the
Very Strange Shipwreck

Twenty-two men fought the raging sea for their lives; but every time they won, they had to fight again.

In the records of Lloyd's of London is the case of the schooner Mermaid and her twenty-two men. Lloyd's has many strange stories in its voluminous files, but nothing to compare with this.

It all began pleasantly enough on the morning of October 16, 1829, when the Mermaid slipped out of the bay at Sydney, bound for Collier Bay, on the west coast of Australia. There was a fair breeze, a bright sun that sparkled from the wave tops, as the Mermaid sliced through them. Aboard ship were eighteen able seamen, three passengers, and Captain Samuel Nolbrow, who had the wheel. Without realizing it, they had all embarked on a voyage that is probably unmatched in the history of the sea.

On the fourth day out of Sydney, the Captain turned the wheel over to the first mate and went below for a wee nip of the stimulants he had thoughtfully provided for himself. The crew lolled about the deck, for they had little to do under the circumstances. The barometer gave no hint of what was to come. It looked like fair weather and smooth

111

sailing, until shortly before two o'clock in the afternoon. Then the vessel found herself becalmed. Thick, gray clouds scudded over the face of the sun.

Alerted by the lack of motion, Captain Nolbrow put away his bottle and stumbled up to the deck again—to find the barometer falling rapidly. Shortly before dark the calm ended with great gusts of wind that soon became a raging gale. The Mermaid fought for her life; for she was in the tortuous Straits of Torres, a narrow channel that had claimed many a ship and many a crew.

The great waves smashed over the bow and boiled around the helmsman, who was lashed to the mast for safety. By the spasmodic flashes of lightning, Captain Nolbrow could see enough to realize that he was fighting a losing battle against the roaring tempest. All hands were on deck when a great wave flung the Mermaid atop a reef that cut her open like a ripe melon. Moments later the twenty-two persons were floundering in the howling darkness.

In all that boiling sea there was but one hope for them, a rocky peak that jutted from the waters about a hundred yards from the sinking vessel. And miracle of miracles, when daylight came—there were twenty-two persons clinging to the rock. Not a life had been lost!

For three cold, wet days they were marooned there—then the bark Swiftsure came pounding through the straits, sighted them, and took them aboard.

All went well for the next five days, until the Swiftsure neared the coast of New Guinea. Then she too fell victim to the jinx that rode her refugee passengers. Without warning, the Swiftsure found herself caught up in a powerful current that did not show on the maps. She was swept broadside into the rocks along the barren coast, and everyone had to abandon ship. And once again, all hands were saved.

Less than eight hours after they had crawled out on the beach, they were rescued—this time by the schooner Governor Ready. It carried thirty-two persons itself, but it managed to make room for the survivors of both the Mermaid and the Swiftsure before it clapped on sail—and sped away down the coast to rendezvous with disaster. Only three hours after the rescue, the Governor Ready caught fire.

Loaded with lumber, the blaze spread rapidly, and the order to abandon ship was given. All aboard piled into the frail longboats with little preparation. Around them lay hundreds of miles of open water, off the regular shipping lanes. Prospects were poor, but their luck was wonderful, for the Australian government cutter Comet came along and picked them up, again without loss of life!

Aboard the Comet there was grumbling, for the crew of the rescue ship regarded the shipwrecked crowd as bearers of a jinx, in spite of their remarkable good fortune which had saved them from death time after time. For exactly one week all went well, and then the Comet ran into a sudden squall that snapped off her mast, ripped away her rails, left her rudderless and at the mercy of the elements. The crew of the Comet got into the only longboat that was still serviceable and pulled away from the doomed vessel, leaving their unwelcome guests to fend for themselves.

For eighteen hours they clung to the wreckage and fought off the sharks; until the packet Jupiter came along and once again snatched them from the jaws of the sea. The Captains called the roll and, for the fourth time, they discovered that throughout the four shipwrecks not a single life had been lost among the entire company!

113

The amazing chronicle has still another odd twist to it. One of the passengers on the Jupiter was an elderly lady, Sarah Richey, of Yorkshire, who was on her way to Australia to search for her son, Peter, who had been missing for fifteen years. She found him, too; for he was among the crewmen of the Mermaid, whom the Jupiter had saved from the sea.

27

The Girl Who Lived Twice

The young girl claimed that she had lived before . . . and the skeptical scientists who put her to the test had to admit defeat. Hers was a case they could neither explain—nor deny!

The middle class parents of Shanti Devi lived quietly in Delhi, India, where she was born in 1926. There was nothing unusual about her birth—nothing at all that might have forewarned her parents of what was to follow.

As she began to grow out of her babyhood, her mother noticed that the child seemed bewildered. She kept to herself and seemed to be carrying on conversations with some imaginary person.

It was not until she was seven years old, however, that her parents became concerned for her sanity; for that was the year that little Shanti told her mother that she had lived before, in a town called Muttra; and she described the house where she claimed to have lived in this alleged earlier existence.

Her mother told Shanti's father; he, in turn, took the child to a physician who questioned her closely. After the child had told her strange story, the doctor could only shake his head. If the little girl was a mental case, she was a most unusual one; and, if not, then he dared not guess at the truth. He advised the father to question the child from time to time and to record the answers; and, if she persisted, to come back and report to him.

Shanti Devi never changed her story. By the time she was nine years old her distracted parents were not surprised at anything she told them, for they had come reluctantly to the belief that she was mentally deranged. It was in 1935 that the girl told her parents that she had lived in Muttra, had been married, and had borne her husband three children. She described the youngsters, gave their names; and claimed that her own name in that previous life had been Ludgi. Her parents only smiled and choked back their grief.

One evening while Shanti and her mother were preparing the evening meal, there was a knock at the door and the girl ran to open it. When she failed to return in a reasonable length of time, her mother began to wonder what was keeping her. She found Shanti staring at a stranger who stood on the steps. The child said, "Mother! This is the cousin of my husband. He lived in the town of Muttra, too, not far from where we lived!"

The man DID live in Muttra, and he had come to talk business with Shanti's father. He did not recognize Shanti; but he told her parents that he had a cousin whose wife, named Ludgi, had died in childbirth ten years before. The worried parents told him the strange story of their daughter's claims; and he agreed to get his cousin to come to Delhi to see if Shanti could recognize him.

The girl was told nothing of the plan; but when the stranger arrived, she threw herself in his arms and sobbed that he was her husband . . . come back to her. The bewildered fellow went with Shanti's parents to the authorities, where they told their incredible story. The government of India appointed a special committee of scientists to investi-

116

gate this case, which was attracting national attention.

Was she really the reincarnation of Ludgi?

The scientists took Shanti to the town of Muttra. As she stepped off the train, she pointed out and correctly named her alleged husband's mother and brother; and she conversed with them in the colloquial dialect of Muttra, although her parents had taught her only Hindustani.

The puzzled scientists continued their test; they blindfolded the girl and put her into a carriage, climbing in beside her. She unhesitatingly directed the driver through the town, described the various landmarks they passed—and finally ordered him to halt at the end of a narrow lane. "This," she said, "is where I lived!" When the bandages were removed from her eyes, she saw the old man who sat smoking in front of the house. "That man was my father-in-law," she told them. And, indeed, he had been the father-in-law of Ludgi!

Oddly, she recognized the two oldest children; but not the youngest, whose birth had cost Ludgi's life.

The scientists were guarded in their comments. They agreed that somehow the child born in Delhi seemed to remember a life in Muttra, and to remember it in amazing detail. The scientists reported that they could find no evidence of trickery and no explanation for what they had seen.

The fully documented story of Shanti Devi, now living quietly as a government employee in New Delhi, is a matter of record in medical and government files. In 1958 she told medical specialists who questioned her that she had learned to adjust herself to living in the present; that the old yearning for her strange past no longer bothered her.

Shanti Devi is living evidence of an enigma that is Stranger Than Science.

28

Target—Earth!

Is the earth headed for destruction? Is there, somewhere out in the void of outer space a gigantic mass of iron which may some day intercept us in one blinding flash? Always a possibility, of course, but is it probable?

Spectacular visitors from space are not infrequent. A meteorite the size of a grapefruit smashed into a home in Syllacauga, Alabama, in 1953 and injured a woman who was asleep on a couch. In 1890 a farmer in Kansas was taking a noon-day nap under his wagon in the hayfield when he was awakened by a brilliant flash . . . a crash like thunder . . . and dirt that flew all around him. Subsequent investigation disclosed that a 188-pound meteorite had buried itself in the earth about sixty feet from where he slept. In 1886, near Cabin Creek, Arkansas, a farm wife was cooking the noon meal when an overwhelming roaring shook the house. She ran out in time to see the tops of several pine trees flying through the air. A 107-pound iron meteorite, which had sheared them off, was found later in a nearby field.

These were mere celestial buckshot compared to the meteoritic mass that ravaged the earth near Winslow, Arizona, some 20,000 years ago. It was in reality a cluster of chunks of iron, some large, some small, weighing in the aggregate many millions of tons. It came crashing in nearly vertically and with such earth-shaking impact that it drove through two thousand feet of solid rock, vaporizing most of its fragments and much of the rock itself. Today, "Meteor Crater" as it is called, is a major tourist attraction, a vast yawning pit about a mile across and six hundred feet deep— evidence of the incalculable fury that results when the earth encounters one of these visitors from space.

Fortunately most of them are quite small, little more than dust. Occasionally one of these bits of iron, the size of a marble, will flash through the atmosphere. But the earth bears scars enough to remind us that we travel a risky road through the universe. For instance, the famed "Bays" of North Carolina and South Carolina, and Northern Georgia . . . oblong-shaped depressions in the earth which were hardly distinguishable until man himself took to the air . . . then they stood revealed for what they were . . . the scars made by a mass of great meteors gouging into the earth as they traveled a course to the southeast, ripping out holes which were in some cases two miles across, and as much as six miles long.

As scientists have reconstructed the scene, a great flaming mass flashed across the midwest, grazed the Blue Ridge Mountains and plowed into the earth at about 150,000 miles an hour. It must have devastated a hundred thousand square miles with its heat and its millions of accompanying meteorites.

Occasionally astronomers will see a tiny star flare briefly into unusual brilliance, possibly the result of collision with some other heavenly body. Is this a preview of the fate that awaits the earth, somewhere along our headlong flight through space? Science cannot say . . . we can only hope our luck will continue to hold out, as it has for billions of years.

29

Saved By A Dream

Is it possible for human beings under great emotional stress to communicate with each other by some mental process which we do not understand? In all the records of such cases, there is none more remarkable than that of a young girl who defied the authorities and believed in her dreams with startling results.

The authorities of Czernak, Poland, regarded the girl as a pest. Time after time she came to them to beg for help to find her boy friend, a young Polish soldier who had marched away to World War I, and vanished, like millions of others, in the fury of battle.

In October of 1918, Merna had her first terrible dream about her missing soldier. She saw him groping his way through a dark tunnel; saw him set down a candle to pit his strength against a jumble of rocks and timbers; and saw him fall sobbing to his knees. Just that—and no more.

Oddly, she had the same dream several times, and then in the middle of the summer of 1919 the scene changed slightly. In the dream she saw a castle on the brow of a hill. One tower of the castle was crumbled into a mass of stones and timbers. As she approached the rubble heap, she heard a voice calling for help! A voice that she instantly recognized as that of Stanislaus, who had been missing for the past year.

The voice was somewhere under that great heap of stones. She tried to lift the stones, but they were too much for her. Sadly she turned away and the dream faded. When the same dream occurred to her time after time, Merna told her mother, and the mother told the village priest. He was understandingly skeptical. He attributed the current night-mares to the mental condition of a heartsick young girl.

But Merna was not to be turned aside so easily. Where was that castle with the crumbled tower? She had no idea, and finding it appeared to be a hopeless task for that part of Europe is replete with castles in varying states of dis-repair—relics of a bygone era.

Time after time those frightful dreams! She saw him fumbling in a tunnel—saw the crumbling castle—heard his pleas for help. Almost penniless, she set out to trudge along the roads of that sector where he had last been seen. A thankless, perhaps an impossible task, for the odds against her were overwhelming. She slept along the roadside. She ate when kindly farmers gave her food. They heard her story and shook their heads. There were so many sad stories from the War; so many old broken down castles—who knows?

On April 25, 1920, she came to the top of a hill near the little village of Zlota in southeast Poland. Merna took one look at the castle that stood on the hilltop above the village—took one look and screamed for joy! There it was! Just as she had seen it in the dream. She ran down the dusty road into the village, tears streaming down her cheeks, and, exhausted, she fell down in the village square beside the fountain. A crowd quickly gathered around her. A local police officer came to ascertain the nature of the excitement. Merna could only point to the castle and babble: "There it is! There it is!"

The gendarme was unimpressed. Of course the castle was there. It had been there for hundreds of years. Why get so excited about it? Merna told her story and nobody believed her. Lovesick girls have been known to do some strange things; perhaps castle hunting was just another of their vagaries. But she attracted so much attention and was so determined to dig in the rubble, that a crowd of the curious went with her.

With tongue in cheek the men set about prying up some of the massive stones. They had been at it for two days when they broke into some sort of opening, and, to their astonishment, they heard a human voice calling to them from the blackness. Merna heard it too. She screamed and tore at the rocks with her hands. The workmen pulled her back and enlarged the opening so that one of them could enter.

They brought out Stanislaus Omensky, pale, ragged, tortured by the light after almost two years in total darkness; but it was he, just as Merna had seen him in her dreams.

He had visited the old castle. An artillery shell had struck a tower and sealed the entrance which he had used, and he had never been able to find another. He had lived off cheese and wine. He found some candles which he used for light, and for companions he had rats—hundreds of them. For hope he had only his prayers.

The astounding climax to Merna's dream was fully confirmed by the investigation of the Polish Army, which naturally wanted to know the details. Stanislaus was eventually dismissed from the service with honors, and he married the girl who had saved his life by her faith in her dreams.

30

Spark of Life?

Did an obscure amateur scientist discover the spark of life? Did Andrew Crosse accidently stumble upon a mixture of chemicals and electricity which produced living things from a lifeless compound? If he did not, then just what did he accomplish? The record of his work is clear—only the enigma of the results remains to plague science.

The neighbors of Andrew Crosse regarded him as more devil than man. They did not understand the bright flashes that lighted his laboratory windows at night when he was tinkering with his crude electrical devices. Not only was he dreaded and shunned as "the thunder and lightning man," but he was denounced as an atheist, a blasphemer, and a Frankenstein who had best be put in chains for the common safety.

Andrew Crosse minded his own business, it is true, but his was a very strange business for the early 1800's. And one of his experiments remains a very strange business to this day.

Andrew was an enthusiastic amateur experimenter in the new field of electricity. Out of touch with others in the same work, he labored under the double handicap of not knowing what had already been done—and of not understanding what he was doing himself. Yet it may have been this very lack of knowledge which led him to undertake the experiments which were to inscribe his name, however faintly, in the annals of science.

He decided to induce the development of artificial crystals by subjecting chemicals to prolonged exposure to weak electrical currents. Andrew mixed up some silicate of potash and hydrochloric acid and into this he dropped a fist-sized chunk of oxide of iron. By inducing the current from a small battery to trickle through the solution to the oxide of iron, he hoped to bring about the growth of artificial crystals of silica.

Having arranged this combination of chemicals and current, Andrew set it aside and went back to his favorite pastime of studying the spark-gap—the flashes which alarmed his neighbors.

Did he accidentally stumble upon an arrangement which created life from inorganic matter?

In a paper which he wrote for the London Electrical Society in that same year of 1837, Andrew set down this account of his experience.

He wrote: "On the fourteenth day after the commencement of this experiment, I observed through a small magnifying lens a few small whitish specks clustered around the middle of the electrified stone. Four days later these specks had doubled in size and had struck out six or eight fine filaments around each speck . . . the filaments longer than the hemisphere from which they projected.

"On the 26th day of the experiment, the objects had assumed the form of perfect insects, standing erect on the bristles which they were growing. Although I regarded this as most unusual I attached no singular significance to it until two days later, the 28th day of the experiment, when the magnifying lens showed that these things were moving their legs. I must say now that I was quite astonished. After a few more days they detached themselves from the stone and moved about through the caustic acid solution.

"In the course of a few weeks more than a hundred of them made their appearance on the oxide of iron. Under a microscope I examined them and found that the smaller ones had six legs, the larger ones had eight. Others who have examined them pronounced them to be of the genus acari, but some say they are an entirely new species.

"I have never ventured an opinion on the cause of their birth for the reason that I have never been able to form one. I thought they might have been airborne creatures that had drifted into the liquid and prospered, but later experiments with closed vessels, in which the ingredients had been purified by baking in the oven, produced identical creatures; therefore, I suggest that they must originate in the electrified liquid by some process unknown to me."

Andrew Crosse realized that he was walking a tightrope before the top scientists of his day. He was describing an experience foreign to their accepted understanding and therefore he was inviting ridicule. He did not have long to wait. Cries of fraud and hoax engulfed him. He and his alleged insects were denounced as nothing more than humbugs.

Amid all the furor that his announcement had created, Crosse stood alone and helpless. Even other scientists who had duplicated his tests with similar results kept their silence.

All but one. That voice was raised in his defense and it

was such a powerful voice that none dared challenge it; for it belonged to the great Michael Faraday. At last Crosse had found his champion.

Faraday reported to the Royal Institution that he too had experienced development of these little creatures in the course of his experiments. But he added that he could not decide whether they had been created in the sterile solutions—or brought back to life by the electricity! Either development would have constituted a milestone in scientific advance, as Faraday realized, but he left it to his fellow scientists to make the decision, if any.

Crosse never claimed to have discovered anything. He was merely reporting what had happened. After the attacks upon him subsided, he retired to his home in the Quontock hills for many more happy years among his test tubes and batteries.

Although he spent his long life as a humble searcher after scientific truths, the contribution for which he is remembered is the controversy over his acari—unwanted then, and unexplained to this day.

31

Giants In The Earth

One of the intriguing puzzles of science is the evidence which supports the Biblical assertion that "there were giants in those days."

For centuries, the Chinese sought out the fossilized remains of extinct dinosaurs and other huge creatures and ground them into powder. This was the stuff of which dragons had been made, they reasoned, and they paid fancy prices for it as a medicine.

In other lands, including our own, the finding of such comparatively recent remains as those of mastodons was frequently misconstrued as skeletal remains of giant humans. On the island of Shemya, out in the Aleutians, mastodon leg bones were pointed out by the natives as evidence that their ancestors had been ponderous fellows, to say the least.

Legends of many races included stories of giant men who once roamed the earth, and an intensive search of scientific records shows that there is physical evidence that supports those legends.

Near Brayton, on the headwaters of the Tennessee River, were found some remarkable footprints, impressed in what is now solid rock. The tracks included those of a human heel ball thirteen inches wide.

The marks showed clearly that the fellow whose stride turned to stone in that distant day also had six toes, and that he was a contemporary of a giant horse-like animal whose hoofprints measured eight by ten inches. The petrified prints, scores of them, indicate that giant men and prehistoric horses existed contemporaneously.

The antiquity of man is further attested by the rock carving in the Supai Canyon in the famed Grand Canyon area, where the Doheny Expedition in 1924 confirmed the existence of a remarkable petroglyph which depicts a dinosaur of the type called *tyrannosaurus rex*, standing erect on his massive tail as he waits for a chance to use his powerful jaws and fangs on a prospective victim.

Dinosaurs were presumably extinct for ages before humans appeared on earth; yet, high up on that canyon wall is this ancient, man-made carving of a dinosaur in action! The carving is so old that the iron, seeping slowly from the stone, has formed its customary protective covering, a task that required untold eons. Scientists are generally agreed that this area where the dinosaur drawing was made has not been under water for forty million years; and the dinosaurs were swamp dwellers. In that same Havasupai Canyon there is another and equally important rock carving which shows a giant human who is either defending himself against a mammoth, or attacking the mammoth. And like the other carving, this one, too, has been coated with the iron patina of the ages.

In late 1958 a human skeleton was found in a layer of coal in an Italian mine . . . a layer that was approximately eleven million years old . . . but he was a comparative newcomer; for in the number three Eagle Coal Mine at Bear Creek, Montana, in November of 1926, miners discovered two huge human molars . . . so large that only a giant could have grown them, and these teeth were in strata at least thirty million years old—old enough that dinosaurs were still roaming the Wyoming swamps when the giant who owned those teeth was alive.

In 1833, soldiers digging a pit for a powder magazine at Lompock Rancho, California, hacked their way through a layer of cemented gravel and came up with the skeleton of a giant man about twelve feet tall. The skeleton was surrounded by carved shells, huge stone axes, and blocks of porphyry covered with unintelligible symbols. The giant was also noteworthy in still another respect: He had a double row of teeth, both upper and lower.

When the natives began to attach some religious significance to the find, authorities ordered the skeleton and all the artifacts secretly reburied—and, of course, lost to the scientific study they deserved.

This particular giant, incidentally, bore marked similarity to another, that of a giant man with double rows of teeth whose skeletal remains were dug up on Santa Rosa Island, off the California coast. Subsequent research has shown that he, or his descendants, feasted on the small elephants which once lived on that island and which have vanished like the giants who ate them, countless ages ago.

Near Crittenden, Arizona, in 1891, workmen excavating for a commercial building came upon a huge stone sarcophagus eight feet below the surface. The contractor called in expert help, and the sarcophagus was opened to reveal a granite mummy case which had once held the body of a human being more than twelve feet tall—a human with six toes, according to the carving of the case. But the body had been buried so many thousands of years that it had long since turned to dust. Just another silent witness to the truth of Genesis, which tells us that there were giants in the earth in those days.

32

Signals From Space

Day after day — hour after hour — the strange signals streamed in from outer space, but who sent them—and why—remain mysteries to all the observatories that recorded them.

The dramatic advent of man-made satellites provided focal points for the giant radio tracking devices. When either Russia or the United States sent an artificial satellite streaking out into orbit around the earth—or beyond—the radio-telescope scientists had field days. Here at last were devices which they could locate and track and identify to their hearts' content.

But in October of 1958 came an event which first brought the usual exuberance and then an aftermath of bewilderment. The scientists tracked the object and recorded its signals before they suddenly realized that they could neither identify the source nor interpret the signals.

Tracking devices at the Cape Canaveral Missile Center in Florida began picking up strong radio signals on the band used by one of the Russian Sputniks. For more than three hours each day the signals poured in—long enough for Canaveral to spread the word among other tracking centers here and abroad.

Within an hour of the time the signals were first detected at Canaveral, other stations were recording them also, and at least two giant radio telescopes in this country alone had located and plotted the apparent position of the device from which the strange signals were emanating.

It was not difficult to determine the position and course of the celestial transmitter. The signals were streaming in from something that was en route to the moon, traveling at an apparent speed in excess of nine thousand miles per hour, although the speed varied considerably if the various calculations were correct.

Up to that point it had seemed probable that the radio signals were routine transmissions from a Russian rocket directed toward the moon. The only factor which cast doubt on that suggestion was the apparent variation in the speed of the thing. No known space rocket would alternately slow down and speed up again as this thing seemed to be doing.

Was it an unannounced Russian lunar probe rocket? The initial complacency of the United States and British scientists was jolted when a check with our world-wide intelligence sources revealed that the Russians had not launched any such devices during the period under observation. Since *we* had not launched anything either during that time period, the riddle deepened. Scientists hastily returned to their recordings and rechecked their involved calculations.

No mistake about it; they had the recordings and they had the flight path of the device from which the signals emanated. It was first noted some 3,000 miles out from the earth, headed on a course which would have taken it to, or near, the moon. Instead, it reduced speed, spurted ahead a couple of times and then seemed to veer off on a new course that would have taken it away from the moon and out into limitless space.

132

The report became common knowledge through the first official releases when the tracking stations proudly announced that they were recording the signals. Confronted with their subsequent confusing discoveries, the official publicity releases hastily sought to cover the premature initial releases.

The customary pattern of multiple-explanation was pursued. This consists of having several allegedly explanatory statements released in rapid sequence, varying in nature but all dealing with the same incident. This achieves the desired goal of creating doubt and confusion while explaining nothing.

In the case of the mysterious radio signals to which we refer, the first of a series of alleged explanations quoted an unnamed Lockheed scientist as saying that the signals, although unidentified, were SIMILAR to those transmitted by Sputnik Number One. Interesting, but meaningless, for Sputnik Number One had been silent for months and had been tracked to its fiery death over the South Atlantic.

An official statement "leaked" to the public through trade papers hinted that ionized gases from rocket exhaust fumes had been tracked to the vicinity of the moon and beyond.

This was a maneuver to indicate, without actually saying so, that the object that had confused the scientists with its signals had been nothing more than a conventional man-made device of some sort. Like the preceding statement from the unnamed Lockheed scientist, it had a fatal flaw. Radio telescopes cannot track any known rocket exhaust fume, ionized or otherwise, from here to the moon.

Signals which do not originate on this earth are not new, of course. Examples are the strange radio signals which

133

Marconi and Tesla reported in the early days of radio—the unexplained geometric light patterns on the moon—the code-like radio chatter from Venus reported in 1956 by Ohio State University and other observatories.

All that is definitely known is that the radio signals in late 1958 came in from something out in space and the signals were recorded for three-hour periods, at a time when no man-made object capable of such signals was in orbit.

What the thing was, where it came from, and where it went are unanswered questions; another chapter in the baffling record of signals from space.

33

The Little People

Was the earth once peopled with races of tiny folk? Does this explain the world-wide distribution of structures and artifacts which seem to have been made by diminutive human beings? Are the legendary fairies nothing more than the mysterious little people of archeology?

Archeologists have long been puzzled by the maze of undersized tunnels and stairways which were found in the pre-Inca ruins of Sachuaman and other South American dawn cities. Tunnels so tiny that children have difficulty negotiating their sharp turns; doorways so small that their use would have been restricted to what we call midgets. Yet, both the tunnels and the doorways bear evidence of use, a great deal of it, for the hard stone from which the passageways were made is deeply worn.

Who were these little people?

Where did they come from?

What happened to them?

At this late date it is unlikely that we shall ever have the answers to those questions, barring some near-miracle discovery of evidence which could provide the clues we need. All that remain are the miles of narrow tunnels cut through solid rock and deeply worn by tiny feet; the artifacts that have been found at various places around the globe, including the beautifully worked little ivory pieces from Shemya, in the Aleutian Islands, and the so-called pigmy flints, perfect arrowheads scarcely half an inch long but unquestionably shaped by human hands.

The tiny hands that made these things have vanished down the trail of time, but the evidence indicates that these people must have been very small, indeed.

To this day there are some scattered races of comparatively small people. The Bushmen of Africa are such a race; fully developed, they average about four feet in height. Some of the Australian aborigines average less than five feet in height, but the smaller members of the tribe appeared to be stunted, perhaps by disease and malnutrition. There are races of small people with us today, but no race of really tiny people; yet, throughout the world there are tens of thousands of very small people who could easily have used the pigmy flints and the undersize tunnels that baffle the scientists.

These diminutives are divided into two categories: The dwarfs, who have normal size trunks and heads, but short arms and legs; and the midgets, who are generally well-formed but much smaller than ordinary folk.

Many of these diminutives have distinguished themselves in every line of worthwhile human endeavor. Charles Third (of Naples), Pepin the Short, Gregory of Tours, the historian Procopious, all were either dwarfs or midgets.

The scourge of Europe, Attila the Hun, was a dwarf. Hussein Pasha, famed for enlightened governmental reforms, was a midget. Aesop, famed for his fables, was a dwarf less than three and a half feet tall. The English painter, Gibson, was exactly three feet tall, as was his wife, but their nine children were all healthy and of normal size. In London in 1742 a noted silversmith named Robert Skinner married a girl his own size and their wedding was the talk of the land because they were only thirty inches tall. Their marriage was blessed with fourteen robust and well-formed children of normal size. At the age of four the children were as tall as their parents.

Most celebrated of the American midgets was Charles Stratton, of Bridgeport, Connecticut, who stopped growing at the age of five months, when he was 21 inches tall—or short. Exhibited by the famed P. T. Barnum under the name of Tom Thumb, the midget amassed a fortune. While presenting Tom Thumb in London, Barnum heard of the wedding of silversmith Robert Skinner and his diminutive bride and determined to emulate it in America. The subsequent marriage of Tom Thumb and Lavinia Warren, a lady of his own stature, was one of the most-talked-about events of the decade, climaxed when the tiny couple were presented to the President and Mrs. Lincoln at the White House.

Probably the tiniest human being ever presented to the public in the United States was a Mexican girl, Lucia Zarete, who is reported to have been seventeen and a half inches tall and who weighed thirteen pounds at the age of twenty. She was smuggled into the United States in an ordinary carpet bag.

From Biblical times to the closing decades of the Middle Ages, dwarfs and midgets were accorded special treatment. Some of the Roman emperors collected dwarfs as other men collect paintings. Cardinal Vitelli gave a banquet in Rome in 1566 at which he had as guests of honor no less than thirty-four dwarfs.

Peter the Great in 1710 had seventy-two of these diminutive folk on the palace staff, using them as special attractions
at state weddings. The most famous English midget, Geoffrey Hudson, was about eighteen inches high at the age of
thirty when he fought a famous duel with a turkey gobbler
that had insulted him by stealing his lunch. Geoffrey won
the duel . . . and ate the gobbler.

34

Mystery In Mid Air

There was always the grim chance that an enemy submarine might sneak into San Francisco Harbor in those dangerous days of 1942. The normal surface patrol had the assistance of navy blimps, slow, ponderous gas-filled bags which carried a normal crew of two on such missions. On this particular morning, the L-8 had sailed away from the blimp base on Treasure Island in good weather for what was expected to be another routine flight to watch the approaches to the bay.

Aboard were two experienced men, Lt. Cody and Ensign Adams. They took off at a few minutes past six. At ten minutes to eight, Lt. Cody radioed to base that he had sighted a sizeable oil slick on the water, suggesting that an enemy submarine might be lurking in the channel. Cody radioed that he was taking the big blimp down to three hundred feet above the water to investigate.

When the two fishing boats in the area saw the blimp circling at such low altitude, they realized that she was looking for a submarine and they sped away to be at a safe distance, in case she began dropping depth bombs. Two patrol boats also stood by at a respectful distance to await the outcome of the investigation.

Instead of dropping her depth bombs, the big blimp suddently soared upward and vanished in the scattered clouds.

Two hours later a couple of fishermen casting from the beach near the Coast Artillery Patrol Station saw the L-8 plunging toward them. As the gondola struck the beach, the fishermen grabbed the tie lines and fought to hold her down. Before the blimp tore loose from them, they noticed that the door of the gondola was open, and there was no one aboard. The L-8 dragged the fishermen along the beach for a hundred yards and then shook them loose.

As she bounced and struck a cliff along the beach, one of her three hundred pound depth bombs broke free and buried itself along a highway. Lightened to this extent, the blimp rose and soared away, to come plunging down half an hour later into the streets of Daly City, a suburb of San Francisco.

A salvage crew dismantled the ship and returned her to the base for inspection which might solve the riddle of the berserk blimp and the missing crew.

A careful investigation showed that everything in the gondola was in order. The rubber lift raft was stowed in place; the parachutes were folded and untouched in their customary shelves. The two bright yellow life jackets were missing, but this was to be expected. It was mandatory to wear them on overwater flights, and they had evidently gone with Cody and Adams—wherever that might be.

A space beneath the deck of the gondola contained no water at all; therefore the Navy experts reasoned that the big blimp had not touched down, however briefly, in the ocean. Had Lt. Cody and his assistant fallen from the blimp as it circled at three hundred feet above the oil slick? Had the sudden loss of their weight caused the blimp to nose up and zoom into the clouds?

It was a plausible supposition, but rather improbable under the circumstances, for the crews of the two patrol boats had been standing by a few hundred yards away, watching every move the L-8 made, and they had seen no officers in bright yellow life jackets falling into the sea, nor had the crews and guests on the nearby fishing boats.

A fall of three hundred feet into the water would have been instantly fatal, of course, had it actually occurred. By the same token, however, the impact would have made a sizeable splash and would surely have torn off one or perhaps both of their inflated yellow life jackets. But no one had seen them fall, no one had seen any such splashes, and an intensive sea and air search turned up no trace of the life jackets or the bodies of the missing officers. The case of Lt. Cody and Ensign Adams was a mystery in 1942 and it remains one to this day.

Missing crews are an old, old story in the annals of the sea, and a classic enigma of a century ago is that of sailing ship, Seabird, out of Honduras for Newport with a load of coffee, expensive hardwoods, pitch pine and dyewoods.

She had been away four months when she appeared one bright Sabbath morning in 1850, sails set, driving toward the reef off Easton's Beach near Newport, Rhode Island. Helpless, the crowd on the beach waited for the ship to meet her doom; instead, a great swell lifted her over the danger zone and sent her scudding onto the beach, unharmed.

When no officers or crew appeared on the Seabird, the watchers waded out and boarded her. The only living thing aboard the vessel was a mongrel dog. Captain John Durham and his crew had vanished. There was coffee boiling in the coffee pot. The instruments were in place. The log book notation showed that the vessel had passed Branton Reef, only a couple of miles offshore from Newport—but in those two miles Captain and crew had vanished without a trace.

A few days later, after the cargo had been removed, the Seabird slipped away in the night—perhaps to join her Captain and crew—for none of them were ever seen again.

35

*The Payless
Pilot*

One of the most successful life savers on record is credited with saving thousands of lives and millions of dollars worth of property; yet he could neither read nor write, and he worked for nothing because he had never heard of money. It would be fitting indeed if we called him Pelorus Jack, the Payless Pilot.

Put yourself in his place.

If you were an excellent navigator would you guide ships through dangerous waters for forty years without being paid for it?

Jack did.

If you were one of the world's best swimmers would you go back to a job where your only reward was a pistol shot in the back?

Jack did.

You see, Pelorus Jack was both a navigator and a swimmer. He worked faithfully at his self-appointed job of guiding ships through dangerous waters for exactly forty years in fair weather and foul, without losing a single ship. No one ever offered to pay him and he never expected to be paid.

Unusual fellow, of course. Most unusual! Pelorus Jack was a porpoise.

Off the coast of New Zealand there is a swift water passage through the D'Urville Islands known as French Pass, which extends from Pelorus Sound to Tasman Bay. It is a short cut—and a dangerous one. Treacherous currents and jagged underwater rocks lie in wait for the hapless and unwary. The pass had a bad reputation among seafaring men—until Pelorus Jack came along. Then, for forty years, it was quite safe, thanks to this remarkable porpoise.

First to make his acquaintance was the schooner Brindle, out of Boston bound for Sydney with a load of machinery and shoes, picking her way gingerly through the Pass one stormy morning in 1871. The crew noticed an unusually large blue-gray porpoise playing along in front of the bows, leaping out of the water and acting like a puppy that is overjoyed at finding a friend.

Some of the crew members mistook the porpoise for a young whale calf and wanted to harpoon it; but the Captain's wife prevented them from carrying out their scheme. By merely groping along through the mist and rain, following the playful porpoise, the Brindle had deep water under her keel all the way through the dangerous pass.

As far as the records are concerned, this trip with the Brindle marked the beginning of Jack's incredible career. Since he hung around Pelorus Sound, waiting to convoy any passing vessel through the pass, he soon acquired the name of Pelorus Jack and his fame spread rapidly around the world, as grateful sailors credited him with providing safe passage for them through those dangerous waters.

For forty years Jack met the ships and leaped out of the water in greeting. Sailors and passengers watched for him and gave him rousing cheers when he appeared, for with Pelorus Jack on the job, the threat of French Pass was nullified. The big porpoise played alongside the vessels, leaping gracefully into the air. He had no difficulty keeping up with the ships, since the porpoise is one of the fastest creatures in the water.

Jack would race alongside the vessels for miles, crossing under them to appear from time to time on the other side, like a sea-going collie herding sheep. But once the craft neared the churning waters of French Pass, Jack would spurt ahead of the bow and remain there, in sight of the pilot, marking the channel until the danger zone was past.

In 1903, a drunken passenger on the Penguin nicked Jack with a pistol bullet. The crew of the ship wanted to lynch the drunk, and had to be forcibly prevented from carrying out their threat. For two weeks Jack failed to report for duty and was presumed to be dead; then, one bright morning he showed up again, the Payless Pilot of French Pass.

The council at Wellington passed an ordinance protecting Jack from molestation, and it was one law that the sailors gladly enforced.

After being shot by the passenger on the Penguin, Jack never met that ship again—the only vessel he refused to accompany. Sailors refused to sign on her; the Penguin was jinxed, they said. At last, left to the resources of only a human pilot, the Penguin piled up on the rocks and sank with heavy loss of life.

To settle the argument whether Jack was porpoise or shark, a group of scientists made numerous trips through the pass, and definitely identified him as a very large porpoise.

145

He was faithful to his self-appointed task but he was getting old. Since he first appeared in 1871, Jack had piloted hundreds of ships through the tortuous waters of French Pass. Not only had he saved thousands of lives, but he had also become world famous.

From his first trip with the Brindle in 1871, Jack was on the job day and night, until April of 1912. Then, as dramatically as he had appeared, Jack vanished. It is probable that he was the victim of age and of his natural enemies. Since he had never trained a successor, his passing left a gap that has gone unfilled.

Pelorus Jack was, as the scientists reported, a remarkable porpoise. He had no predecessor—and no successor. But he does have a record of life saving unequalled in the annals of the sea.

36

The Case of the
Missing Corpse

In the Huguenot Museum at Cape Town, South Africa, is a tombstone bearing the name of a young man who warned authorities that they might take his life . . . but they could not keep his body . . . and events proved him right!

As Father Dupre entered his cell the prisoner in the death cell at Cape Province Prison stood up. Two soldiers were on guard at the door. The condemned man slowly reached out and took the Bible from the priest's hand . . . "This is my book and my life" . . . he said. . . . "I lived by it . . . and I swear before God that I did not kill Pierre Villiers. I go to my death an innocent man."

The priest put his hands on the boy's shoulders. "I believe you, my son," he said, "but they have decreed that you must be hanged this morning."

A moment later the Governor of the Cape Province Penitentiary stepped into the cell and read the formal document which reminded the doomed man that he, John Gebhard, had been sentenced to hang for the murder of Pierre Villiers, a farm laborer, whom he had been convicted of strangling. Did Gebhard have anything to say? The prisoner replied . . . "Yes! I am innocent!"

On that bright morning in November, 1856, John Gebhard walked the short distance to the gallows with firm
step. He stood without visible emotion beside the swaying
noose that would soon snuff out his life. As Father Dupre
started to read the customary burial service, Gebhard
turned to him and said, "Father, don't bother to waste your
time on that. . . . They may destroy this body of mine . . .
but they cannot kill my soul!"

By this time the executioner had slipped the heavy noose
over the prisoner's head and pulled the knot up behind his
ear. Gebhard had only seconds to live. He twisted his head
around in the black hood and said, "No grave shall hold
me! You hear? No grave shall hold me! You can't keep me
in a grave, because I die an innocent man. . . ."

There was a click as the trap released, and John Gebhard
swung off into eternity.

About two hours later, after the necessary medical examination and the legal determination that he was dead, as
decreed by law, his body was placed in a plain black coffin.
Because of the widespread attention the case had attracted,
authorities at the prison made doubly sure that the coffin
lid was heavily nailed into place and the lid sealed down
before the prison guards placed it in a cart for burial on
the slopes of Paarl Mountain, behind the prison.

The guards placed the box in a grave eight feet deep and
covered it with a cairn of stones. In accordance with the
instructions from the Governor, armed guards stood watch
over the grave, day and night, for two months, to thwart
any attempts to remove the body.

Other events were taking shape which were to give this
unusual case a new turn. At the farm where John Gebhard
had been accused of killing Pierre Villiers, the owner dis-

covered the purse of the murder victim in the possession of one of the ranch hands, Peter Lorenz. When Lorenz tried to flee, he was caught and held for police. Search of his bunk also revealed that he had the ring and watch of the unfortunate Pierre Villiers. Lorenz subsequently babbled out his confession: *He* had murdered Villiers . . . and *he* had been the principal witness whose testimony had put the rope around the neck of John Gebhard.

There had indeed been a tragic miscarriage of justice—John Gebhard had gone to the gallows for a crime he had not committed. The Governor of the Province of Good Hope ordered Gebhard's name cleared of the crime, and an immediate payment of 1,000 pounds to the widowed mother of the unjustly executed man. She was also to receive a pension of 108 pounds per year for the balance of her life.

The Governor also ordered that the body of John Gebhard be exhumed and reburied in consecrated ground at the expense of the government.

Mrs. Gebhard accompanied the official group which climbed the slopes of Paarl Mountain to the spot where her son had been buried only two months before. She stood by as the soldiers removed the stones and the earth, and finally brought the coffin to the surface. The prison governor examined the coffin and found the seals in order. The guards pried off the lid—but the box was empty!

Subsequent official investigation disclosed that his grave had not gone unguarded for a moment during the period between his burial and the startling discovery that his coffin was empty. The government dug up scores of other graves in the vicinity, without result. John Gebhard's body could not be found.

Almost a century later, in August of 1956, some picnickers found a heavy black marble slab high on the slopes of Paarl Mountain. It was lying face down, and was covered with writing. The inscription reads . . . "Sacred to the memory of John Gebhard. Blessed are they that rest in the Lord." That slab is now in the museum at Paarl, Cape Town; a lasting reminder of John Gebhard's claim that no grave could hold him.

37

Mental Marvels

Most television audiences are familiar with performances given by persons who are introduced as having so-called "photographic minds"—persons who glance at the pages of books and magazines and then describe the contents, page by page. Is it fraud—or fact?

The incredible powers of the human mind are demonstrated in many ways; the well-documented ability to defy time and space through the act of dreaming; the ability to reason to the extent of studying the mind itself; the ability to separate the conscious mind from the unconscious; the well-known but little understood ability to function as a fantastically retentive storehouse and, in some cases, as a calculating machine.

Somewhere in this complex of remarkable endowment lies the explanation of the television performers with the photographic minds. It is there—but thus far no scientist has been able to explain it beyond reiterating the well-known fact that the subconscious mind forgets little or nothing; it remains only to develop the ability to recall from the subconscious to be able to perform amazing feats of memory.

Perhaps the best known case of such fabulous ability

to memorize was the Rabbi Elijah of Vilna, a Lithuanian, who regarded his strange mental power as a curse. During his lifetime he read, and memorized at one reading, more than two thousand volumes. At will he could recall any page and any portion of any page in any of those books. From his viewpoint the ability was undesirable because he was unable to forget anything that he had read. It was, as he described it, like living in a library all day and taking it to bed with you at night.

The renowned French statesman, Leon Gambetta, was endowed with a remarkable memory comparable to that of Rabbi Elijah. Gambetta could repeat verbatim thousands of pages of the works of Victor Hugo and he could repeat the works forward or backward, beginning at any desired point in the volume. The famous Greek scholar, Richard Porson, shared this unusual ability to the extent that he was able to quote page after page from almost any book he had ever read.

It was another amazingly retentive memory that enabled Harry Nelson Pillsbury to win for himself the title of American chess wizard. His uncanny ability to remember the precise locations of every chessman on as many as twenty boards at a time plus the ability to recall more than a thousand moves that had been made enabled him to play as many as twenty blindfold games simultaneously. Sometimes, just to relieve the tedium of the chess match, he would play a blindfold game of cards at the same time as the chess matches.

Mathurin Veyssiere, who was the librarian to the King of Prussia, had an incredible memory for sound. After once hearing a sentence spoken in any language he could repeat the sentence with the proper pronunciation and the original accent. On one test of his powers, twelve foreign emissaries, each speaking a different language, delivered twelve sentences which Veyssiere heard and when they had finished, repeated to them correctly.

The ability to perform prodigious mathematical feats mentally is a rare but well-documented endowment of persons known as human calculating machines.

One such marvel was a retiring chap named Zerah Colburn of Vermont. As a child he attracted attention by his surprising proclivity to solve involved mathematical problems in his mind. At the age of eight he was taken to London where the learned men might observe at close range this gifted lad. They put him through intensive tests which only left them more baffled than ever, for Zerah Colburn did not even know the rules of simple arithmetic, yet he unhesitatingly gave them almost instantaneous answers to such problems as that of extracting the cube root of 268, 336, 125, while at the same time he was raising 8 to the 16th power!

During his tests in London, the child was asked by the Duke of Gloucester to explain the method by which he had just multiplied 21,735 by 543 and the youngster promptly replied: "I simply multiplied 65,205 by 181!" The boy had the correct answer, but like the puzzled professors, he could not explain the process.

When Jedidiah Buxton dallied on his problems for hours or months—Johann Martin Dase delivered the answers in seconds or minutes. Born in Hamburg in 1824, he was considered so reliable that scientists of his day often asked Dase to solve their involved astronomical computations. He once multiplied a number of 100 digits by a similar number in nine minutes . . . which is about twice as fast as the modern electronic brains can do the same job.

If they prove anything else, the careers of these prodigies prove that the human mind is a wonderland of incredible capabilities, little understood and largely unexplained.

38

Genius In Revolt

A life story that ranges from being a genius at four to being a failure at forty—that was the story of William Sidis. And strangest of all, he was a failure by choice.

At the tender age of two, little William could read high school text books, a logical stage of development for a youngster who had been able to select any letter of the alphabet when he was six months old. On his fourth birthday, under orders from his father, the child wrote two five-hundred-word treatises, one in French and the other in English.

A year later, while the father beamed with pride at this genius he had shaped, little William Sidis observed his birthday with another mental milestone; he wrote a profound treatise on anatomy. Professor Boris Sidis took the treatise to Harvard University to show his learned colleagues what his remarkable child had accomplished and they were properly surprised but the child had still another marvel in store for *them,* as well as his father. Young Sidis revealed that he had worked out a method of calculating the day of the week on which any day had fallen. His method worked, too, as far back as ten thousand years, the scholars learned.

By the time he was ten, the child had written a text book on geometry—and had written it in Greek. At eleven he was a student at Harvard. He had been qualified two years earlier, but the authorities at the university felt that he should wait a bit before enrolling.

Genius at two—an embittered failure at twenty! What happened?

The chronological sequence of events in his life gives us many clues but no definitive answer.

Boris Sidis taught abnormal psychology at Harvard. He is known as the brilliant author of several volumes dealing with the subject he taught, and is well remembered as an honored member of the Harvard staff. Dr. Sidis made a fateful decision shortly prior to the arrival of his son; he decided to put some of his theories on mental development to the test by using his own child as the guinea pig. Thereby he ruined two lives.

It was the father's contention that the brain could be developed just as muscles are developed—by getting an early start and forcing the work load.

When little William arrived, his future was figuratively perched on the edge of his crib. The austere father had suspended the letters of the alphabet on strings over the baby's bed. Several times each day he showed the letters to the infant, calling out their names as he did so. Hour after hour this continued, and day after day. Small wonder that by the time William Sidis was six months old he could identify the letters.

So far, so good—but what next?

None of those silly nursery rhymes, declared Sidis senior. Instead, the child was bombarded every day with textbooks. Geography, geometry, physiology, and Greek

156

were the daily fare of the hapless youngster. He was permitted no playmates. His world was a prefabricated playhouse of the abstruse. Month by month his incredible mental development continued, to the amazement of his father's colleagues and to the bewilderment of his helpless mother.

Brilliant though he was, the elder Sidis had a serious blind spot. By the time his son was eight years old, the boy had developed a strange habit of giggling at inappropriate moments, a hysterical reaction that popped out when the child was involved in the weightiest mental problems. It was a sign of disaster which the father failed to recognize.

The high point of this program of forced mental feeding was reached when William was fourteen, on the day he took the lecture rostrum at Harvard to discourse to the learned men of 1912 on the Fourth Dimension. As he concluded his speech, and with their applause ringing in his ears, the teen-age genius turned from the lectern giggling hysterically and uncontrollably.

After a lengthy stay in a sanitarium at Portsmouth, New Hampshire, the boy came back to Harvard and graduated with honors. He told newsmen that all he wanted of life was a chance to live a normal existence. William Sidis had called a halt on his father's experiment.

He became a teacher at Rice Institute in Houston, only to learn that he did not know how to get along with people. Both in and out of school they shunned him. Now in full revolt against his father and the world, he was convicted of inciting a May Day riot and drew an eighteen-month suspended sentence.

For months he simply vanished, until an old friend of his father's chanced upon the young man clerking in a store under an assumed name for twenty-three dollars a week. From the heights of genius, he sank to the Skid Roads of society. Under persistent pressure from an old acquaintance, Sidis agreed to make a public address on the subject of probable life on Mars. Instead, he discoursed for more than an hour, interrupted by fits of giggling, on the subject of street car transfers.

In the summer of 1944, a world at war took little notice of the unkempt man who died of pneumonia in a Brookline boarding house. The substantial inheritance from his father had gone untouched. To the bitter end, Genius William Sidis refused to touch the money of the parent who had ruined his mind.

39

Wyoming's Mystery Mummy

One of the world's tiniest mummies, and one of archeology's biggest mysteries is the mummy of a man only fourteen inches tall—so ancient that no counterpart has ever been found.

Scientists from far and near have examined this tiny fellow and have gone away amazed. He is unlike anything they ever saw before. Sitting there on the shelf in Casper, Wyoming, visible, disturbing evidence that science may have overlooked him and his kind much too long.

In October of 1932 a couple of gold prospectors were working a gulch at the base of the Pedro mountains about sixty miles west of Casper. They had found some "color" in the solid stone wall of the gulch; they set an extra heavy charge to rip deeper into the stone.

The powerful blast exposed a small natural cave in the solid granite, a cave not more than four feet wide, four feet high and possibly fifteen feet deep.

When the smoke and dust had settled, the miners got down and peered into the opening, and got the shock of their lives; for there, peering right back at them, was a tiny mummy of a man-like creature.

He was on a tiny ledge, legs crossed, sitting on his feet,

159

arms folded in his lap. He was dark brown, deeply wrinkled, with a face that was almost monkey-like in some respects. One eye had a definite droop as though this strange little fellow might be winking at those who found him.

The prospectors carefully picked him up, wrapped him in a blanket and headed back for Casper, where the news of their discovery attracted considerable attention. Scientists were skeptical, but interested; for according to conventional archeology it would be impossible for a living being to be entombed in solid granite. But there it was, in defiance of orthodoxy.

Perhaps it wasn't a living creature . . . a hoax perhaps . . . the X-ray would tell, of course. And an X-ray did tell. It showed unmistakably that here was a creature that had been a man, or man-like. Its tiny skull, the vertebrae of its spine, the rib cage, the bones of the arms and legs were readily discernible.

The little fellow had been about fourteen inches tall in life. Mummified, he weighs about twelve ounces. His features have developed an overall bronze-like hue. The forehead is very low, the nose flat with widespread nostrils, the mouth very wide with thin twisted lips set in a sardonic half grin.

The X-rays show a full set of teeth. Biologists who have examined it declare that the creature was about sixty-five years old at time of death. And when did that occur? Nobody knows, and no scientist thus far has ventured an opinion.

The Anthropological Department of Harvard says there is no doubt of the genuineness of the mummy. Dr. Henry Shapiro, head of the Anthropology Department of the American Museum of Natural History, said that the X-rays revealed a very small skeletal structure covered by dried skin, obviously of extremely great age, historically speaking, and of unknown type and origin. The mystery mummy, said Dr. Shapiro, is much smaller than any human types now known to man.

Is it the body of a mummified infant? Anthropologists who have examined it are of the opinion that, whatever it is, it was full grown at the time of death. The curator of the Boston Museum Egyptian Department examined the creature and declared that it had the appearance of Egyptian mummies which had not been wrapped to prevent exposure to the air. Still another expert, Dr. Henry Fairfield, ventured the supposition that the mystery mummy of the Pedro Mountains might be a form of anthropoid which roamed the North American continent about the middle of the Pliocene Age.

It was natural that the cave itself should be subjected to careful investigation. Scientists found no traces of any human residence there, no artifacts, no carvings or writings —nothing but the tiny stone ledge on which this mummy had been sitting for countless ages. Possibly he was a remarkable curiosity even in his own time and among his own kind, whatever that may have been.

Nature occasionally turns out some very small specimens and this creature may have been one—an early human in unbelievable miniature, possibly held in awe by his fellows for that reason. This might account for his unusual interment by a race that ordinarily treated its dead with less attention.

The only other mummified midget discovered in this country was a red-haired mummy found on a ledge in Mammoth Cave, Kentucky, in the 1920's, a runt about three feet tall who showed signs of being only a few hundred years dead, at most.

The mystery mummy of the Pedro Mountains has never been explained, and may never be; for he presents the experts with some possibilities at variance with their accepted theories.

They are quite content to leave him on display in Casper, Wyoming, an unexplained relic of the dawn of man.

40

The Cursed Car

It was an elaborate automobile, and it figured in the deaths of 20 million people before fate finally caught up with it.

The bright red six-passenger touring car had been driven less than two hundred miles when it carried two members of royalty to their tragic rendezvous. In fact, the car had been built especially for their service when they visited the tiny Bosnian capital of Sarajevo. The date was June 28, 1914. The political situation throughout Europe was explosive; all that was needed was a spark to touch off the war that awaited only an excuse.

Archduke Franz Ferdinand and his wife, the Duchess of Hohenburg, entered the brand-new bright red phaeton to drive through the streets of Sarajevo. For some reason which was never ascertained, they did not turn back when a bomb was thrown at the car.

The bomb struck the side and bounced back into the street. The explosion injured four members of the Archduke's staff who were riding horseback behind the car. After seeing that the injured had been cared for, the royal couple proceeded with their tour of the small city.

Enter unexplained factor number two. Their driver,

who was thoroughly familiar with the city, left the pre-arranged route and drove the bright red car into a dead-end street. A young man, waving a pistol and shouting maledictions, sprang out of a doorway on the narrow street and jumped onto the running board of the car, firing shot after shot at point blank range into the bodies of the Archduke and the Duchess. They were dead by the time the astounded guards could beat the assassin to the cobblestones.

The murder of this royal couple was the spark that touched off World War I with a total loss of twenty million lives. Behind the cataclysm, the evil red car continued to blight the lives of those who came into contact with it.

A week after the war burst over Europe, General Potiorek, distinguished Commander of the Fifth Austrian Corps, seized the Governor's house at Sarajevo and with it he came into possession of the car with the curse.

He did not have long to wait. Twenty-one days later he suffered a catastrophic defeat at Valievo, lost his command and was sent back to Vienna where he became an impoverished lunatic who eventually died in the almshouse.

The red car was taken over by another Austrian, a Captain who had been on the ill-fated Potiorek's staff. The Captain and the curse came together quickly. Driving at high speed, he struck and killed two Croatian peasants, swerved into a tree and was dead when troops removed him from the wreck. The Captain had had the car nine days.

After the Armistice, the newly appointed Governor of Yugoslavia became the owner of the car, which he ordered restored to first-class condition. He was involved in four accidents in four months, in the fourth of which he lost his right arm.

The Governor ordered the car destroyed, for its evil reputation was so well known that it seemed unlikely anyone would want to drive it. But a prospect appeared, a Doctor Srkis, who laughed at the alleged curse. He bought the car for virtually nothing. Unable to secure a chauffeur, the medic decided to drive the car himself.

He was quite happy with it for six months and the results seemed to support his contention that the curse was nothing more than a figment of the public imagination. Then one morning the car was found upside down beside the road, only slightly damaged, the Doctor's body beside it. He had been crushed to death when car rolled over on him.

The Doctor's widow sold the car to a wealthy jeweler who enjoyed it for a year . . . until he committed suicide. The next owner was another doctor whose patients deserted him, fearful of the curse on the car. He unloaded it on a Swiss race driver who entered a road race in the Dolomites, where it threw him over a stone wall to his death.

Back to a well-to-do farmer near Sarajevo it went. He had it repaired, drove it without incident for months. Then one morning it stopped on the road. He induced a passing farmer to tie it on behind his cart for a tow-in to the city. They had scarcely started when the car roared into power, knocked the cart and horses aside, and careened down the road, killing its owner as it overturned on a sharp bend.

But its grisly trail was coming to an end. The battered red car was bought by Tiber Hirshfield, a garage owner, who repaired it and painted it blue. Unable to sell it, he drove it himself. One day when he was taking six friends to a wedding he tried to pass another car at high speed.

Hirshfield and four companions were killed.

The car was rebuilt at government expense and sent to a Vienna museum.

It had killed 16 persons. It had helped to start one world war; and it remained for another war to destroy it—for the curse of the red car was ended by an Allied bomb during World War II.

41

Oddest Spot
on Earth

The moment you see the place, something tells you that nature has gone mad. If you are on horseback the horse will instinctively shy away from it. Birds suddenly swing about in flight and dart away to less disturbing scenes. Even the trees give the impression that they, too, are under the influence of a power they cannot escape; for *within* that strange circle of gravitational insanity, the tree limbs droop noticeably and the trees themselves lean toward the magnetic north, although the trees around them point straight up.

This is the world famed "Oregon Vortex." It lies along the banks of Sardine Creek about thirty miles from Grant's Pass, Oregon. What it *does* is well known but *why* and *how* are questions unanswered.

The vortex is approximately 165 feet in diameter. It is roughly circular in shape, but instruments indicate that the exact size of the tormented zone varies slightly from time to time at ninety-day intervals. Within this circle is an old wooden shed, once an assay office but abandoned back about 1890 when the scales began to play tricks. At that time the building was uphill, about 40 feet outside the limits of the vortex. After the shack was abandoned, that portion of the hill slid down to its present position.

The building itself is warped and twisted; whether by the unknown forces of the vortex or from the strain of sliding down the hill is a matter of conjecture.

When you step inside the old building you're in another world of sorts. You feel a tremendous pull downward, as though gravity had suddenly been intensified. You instinctively lean at an angle of about ten degrees toward the center of the circle. If you lean backward, that is, toward the outside of the circle, you have a creepy feeling of being pulled toward its center—as instruments indicate that you are.

Many scientists have conducted lengthy experiments at the vortex, trying to unravel its riddle. They hung a 28-pound steel ball on a chain from a beam in the old shack. Visitors see this ball apparently hanging at an angle, defying the laws of gravity. It dangles perceptibly toward the center of the circle. You can easily push it in *that* direction, but it is more difficult to shove it toward the *rim* of the circle.

Even cigarette smoke is affected by the weird forces within the vortex. A puff of smoke blown into the still air within the shack will begin to spiral, faster and faster, until it vanishes.

Some of the uncanny antics that startle the tourists include such experiments as placing an empty glass jar on a sloping board, and watching it roll uphill. A ball, even a child's sponge rubber ball, placed on a level spot on the earth near the *edge* of the circle will invariably roll slowly toward the center of the vortex. A handful of tiny paper scraps tossed into the air will spiral madly about as though stirred in mid air by some unseen hand. It is a creepy sensation in an eerie setting.

This remote woodland glade where nature seems to have gone mad was known to the Indians, who solemnly assured the early white settlers that the place was cursed. The palefaces had to be shown, and having been shown, they had to investigate; as they are still doing to this very day.

Is it merely an optical illusion accompanied by vivid imagination?

Instruments have been used which measured the outer limits of the disturbance and determined the size of the circle as roughly 165 feet. Other instruments were carefully set up, beyond the influence of the vortex itself. By sighting thru the planes of these devices it was easy to establish that the feeling of standing at an angle *within* the circle was *not* imaginary.

By the same method it was easy to prove that the 28-pound steel ball suspended from the chain inside the shack actually *DOES* hang at an angle toward the center of the vortex. Golf clubs, brooms and other odds and ends of that general configuration are easy to stand on end inside the confines of the freakish circle; and, in order to be balanced, they must be leaned at a measurable angle away from the center of the vortex.

The phenomenon which accompanies the vortex forces is demonstrably electro-magnetic in character.

An ordinary photographer's light meter, which converts light into electricity and registers it on a dial, will show wide variation between the daylight inside the circle and that beyond its limits. Compasses simply refuse to function.

The world famed Oregon Vortex is similar in some respects to another spot about forty-five miles away in the

Siskiyou Mountains, although the phenomenon at the Vortex is much more profound. At Camp Burch, Colorado, still another magnetic sink seems to operate, again less powerful than the Vortex.

The force is there. It is measurable, but *what* it is or *why* it is nobody knows. The Oregon Vortex is indeed the oddest —and perhaps the "craziest" spot on earth.

42

High Voltage
Humans

Rare, and unexplainable, are those strange people who seem to be charged with high voltage electricity. Medical science doesn't know what to make of them, so it does the next best thing . . . it proceeds to forget them.

For instance—

Dr. Ashcraft doubted the stories he had been hearing about the young girl's charge of high voltage electricity, so he reached out and took her by the hand. A few moments later, when he opened his eyes, the doubting doctor found himself on his back, surrounded by a group of worried friends. Jennie Moran had done it again.

She lived near Sedalia, Missouri, in 1895, a frail, nervous girl then in her middle teens. The phenomenon which attracted so much attention to her was not noticeably present until she was about fourteen years old. Then, for no apparent reason, Jennie suddenly behaved like a powerful storage battery. Sparks flew from her finger tips when she reached for the pump handle, and the voltage was so high that the spark was painful to her. The sparks were doubly painful to anyone who chanced to touch her under conditions which enabled the electricity to leap through their bodies.

Needless to say, Jennie had few close friends. She regarded the phenomenon as a curse, principally because the family cat was one of her favorite pets and the cat avoided her like the plague after it had received a few shocks.

Jennie's strange electrical endowment faded by the time she reached maturity, and she became another normal young woman, much to her delight.

Medical and newspaper records tell of another human storage battery in the person of Caroline Clare, of Bondon, Ontario. In 1877, when she was seventeen years old, Caroline was a strapping 130-pounder who lived with her parents and six brothers and sisters. She became ill, lost her appetite and began to waste away. Doctors could find nothing seriously wrong with her, but she continued to dwindle until her weight dropped to slightly less than ninety pounds.

Then she underwent a mental change as drastic and as baffling as the physical change had been, for Caroline began suffering from seizures—or convulsions—as some of the doctors described them. While in this state, body rigid, eyes fixed and staring, she would mumble at great length of far away places and scenes which she had never visited. It made no sense to those who knew her, for this simple child had hardly been outside her native town.

For a year and a half Caroline remained in this condition before she took a turn for the better, but it was not an unmixed blessing, for when her physical and mental health returned to normal, she discovered that she had acquired an unwanted propensity for shocking people who merely touched her. Oddly enough, she not only emitted considerable voltage, but she seemed to be magnetized as well, for when she picked up any metal article susceptible to magnetic attraction, she could not let go of it; someone had to forcibly pull the article from her open hand.

As in the case of Jennie Morgan, the curse of the annoying electrical charge left Caroline when she reached maturity, simply fading gradually, to return no more. Her case was studied by physicians and a report made to the Ontario Medical Association in the summer of 1879.

In 1890 sixteen-year-old Louis Hamburger came to the Maryland College of Pharmacy, where his unusual ability to act as a human magnet soon attracted the attention of the faculty. Those gentlemen felt the need for more highly trained investigators, so they invited various medical and electrical experts to view this remarkable young man. Their report indicated that they were quite baffled by Louis Hamburger's ability to make heavy iron or steel objects dangle from his fingertips as though from a powerful magnet. Metal rods half an inch in diameter and a foot long were no problem at all; and, when iron filings were placed in a glass beaker, Louis could lift the beaker with the tips of three fingers pressed against the glass. When one of the finger tips was pulled away it caused an audible click.

The electrical phenomenon which jinxed Jennie Moran and Caroline Clare and Louis Hamburger was similar in a general way to that which plagued Frank McKinstry of Joplin, Missouri, around 1889. Similar to the extent that, like the others, the phenomenon was not subject to his will and the voltage was at its peak in the morning after he had had a good night's rest; fading gradually as the day wore on.

On cold days, especially, when most people are subject

to accumulations of static electricity, McKinstry had the unfortunate faculty of becoming so heavily charged that walking became a task, as though he were treading on fly paper. He, too, was investigated and forgotten, for in all these cases science admittedly found only the evidence . . . but not the answers.

43

Britain's Mystery Mile

Motorist after motorist had skidded to a stop after their windshields were shattered by the Phantom Sniper. . . . There were the bullet holes . . . but there was the mystery . . . too . . . and so it remains. . . .

According to police records, the first motorist whose windshield was shattered on that same stretch of road reported his unnerving experience in March of 1951, the first of thirty-two such reports the worried gendarmes received in the ensuing sixteen months.

The experience of Thomas Woods of York Road, Kingston, Surrey, is typical of the lot. On April 3, 1952, a bit after four-thirty in the afternoon, Thomas was driving his truck between Cobham and Esher, on the road from London to Portsmouth. Traffic was almost non-existent; the only other vehicle in sight was another truck about a hundred yards in front of him.

Suddenly his windshield shattered and glass flew back on the front seat. There, perhaps a foot to the left of his head, was a hole through the glass large enough for Thomas to stick his fist through had he cared to try. Thomas noted the spot where all this had happened and headed for the nearest police post to report.

Said he, "I find this to be quite unsettling!"

Truck driver Thomas Woods was expressing the feeling of the scores of motorists who have shared his experience, both before and since.

Strangely, the phantom bullets always find their marks in one straight stretch of road about two and half miles long. It is smooth, there is no speed limit on it, the fields alongside the highway are open, with the exception of a few small bushes where no gunman could hide. But time after time there is a flash, a crash, and the windshields are perforated with holes similar to those which might be made by a very small high-powered rifle.

So far so good. . . .

As the reports came in, time after time, the perplexed police felt encouraged. Take the case of Mr. and Mrs. Eric Sykes, on May 8, 1952. They were driving along at a modest forty miles per hour near Esher Common when there was a bright flash as though a firecracker had exploded on their windshield, a bang like a gunshot, and their windshield was cobwebbed with hairline cracks radiating from a hole about the diameter of a lead pencil. Eric slid to a stop, he and his wife leaped out and looked around for their assailant, and saw nothing except the open, rolling fields, and not a car in sight.

After about a year of these baffling experiences, the police theorized that some gun crank with a high-powered rifle was haunting the roadside along that stretch of highway, firing through motorists' windshields, a dangerous prank that must inevitably end in tragedy.

It was a good theory, but that's all it was. The objects that cracked the windshields came from many angles, but they vanished when they struck the windshields. They

176

never fell inside the cars nor did they ever go on through the cars.

Gun experts admitted that under test conditions it might be possible to create such an effect by using frangible bullets that would disintegrate on impact, but only at very short distances and certainly not on a moving target carrying passengers down a public highway. But even that theory fell by the wayside when microscopic examination of the bullet holes, including one in the metal door of a car, failed to produce any evidence that frangible bullets had been used.

While the worried police were setting traps and studying reports of the phantom bullets of the Portland road, the phenomenon changed its locale, it moved right into the town of Esher itself, where on June 16, 1952, a shop window in Station Road was neatly holed and four days later an angry tavern keeper reported to police that he too had been a victim; there was a small round hole in a front window of his tavern, identical to those in the motorists' windshields.

Whoever, or whatever, was responsible for the phantom bullet holes was internationally inclined; for, in June of 1952, State police in both Indiana and Illinois found themselves chasing a phantom gunman who was fully as elusive as the one in England.

The luckless American motorists, like their British counterparts, saw nothing, heard nothing, except the flash on the windshield, the bang, the splintered glass that showered inside the car. And again, no bullet was ever found inside the cars; and no hole where it might have gone on through the vehicle.

Science was baffled; but not without a suggestion. For

it is known that a meteorite the size of a pinhead traveling at incredible speed would produce precisely the effects attributed to the phantom bullets. Possible? Yes, said science, but not under the known circumstances.

So another theory was filed away. Only the shattered windshields—and the riddle remain.

44

The Enigma of Dighton Rock

For almost three hundred years the story carved into the face of Dighton Rock has defied the best efforts of scholars.

If the latest attempt to decipher it proves to be the correct one, history will have added a new and fascinating chapter.

The writing on Dighton Rock has been there for centuries; no mistake about that. Someone spent many months with a metal tool of some unknown type, hammering the message, whatever it is, into the hard stone surface that shows above tidewater at the junction of Taunton River at Assonet Neck, Massachusetts.

Best seen when the sunlight glances obliquely across its face, the writing on Dighton Rock has been a subject of controversy and wonder since 1690.

In that year the redoubtable Cotton Mather wrote, "Among the curiosities of New England is that of a mighty rock, covered in part at high tide. On a perpendicular side thereof there are very deeply engraved, no man alive knows how or when, about a half score lines, near ten feet long, and a foot and a half broad, filled with strange characters which would suggest as odd thoughts about them that were

179

here before us, as there are odd shapes in that elaborate monument."

From Cotton Mather's day to our own, speculation as to the origin and purpose of the carvings has been rife, and richly endowed with imaginative proposals.

First to go on record with a possible solution to the mystery of the writing on Dighton Rock was Count De Gebelin of Paris, who came and marveled and went away to ponder. The Count later declared that he had fathomed the meaning of the rock writing. Sailors from ancient Carthage, he said, who lived among the Indians on the Massachusetts shore for a time were telling how they consulted an oracle for advice on when to leave for Carthage. It was an interesting supposition, but unsupportable.

In 1807, Samuel Harris, Junior, of Harvard delivered a different interpretation of the same writing. Unmistakably ancient Hebrew, said the Harvard savant. He professed to see Phoenician letters indicating priest, king and idol.

There the puzzle rested for twenty-four years, until Ira Hill, a Maryland schoolteacher who was intrigued by the strange carvings, divested himself of still another "explanation." He called attention to a passage in the Old Testament telling how Hiram and Solomon had sent out an expedition to bring gold from Ophir. The carvings of Dighton Rock, said Mr. Hill, tell the story of this Biblical expedition, which started for Ophir and somehow wandered to Massachusetts instead.

Fortunately for later scholars, a minister made a careful sketch of the carvings in 1690 and this sketch enables students of the present to fill in where vandals and the ravages of wind and wave have made erasures in the intervening centuries.

All are agreed that the marks are deliberate carvings of considerable age, painstakingly and laboriously done for a purpose presently unknown. In view of the physical requirements for carving such hard stone, there is little likelihood that they could be of Indian origin. It is also worth noting that the carvings are engraved on the side of the rock facing the sea, where they would be readily seen by any vessel that ventured into the anchorage in search of shelter or of drinking water.

In 1837, a Danish scholar, Carl Rafn, published a study of the enigma, a document in which he sought to link the writings with a recorded trip of Leif the Lucky, who sailed in the year 1000 to the shores of the North American continent.

On Dighton Rock, said Rafn, he and his colleagues had traced out the Norse characters which described a conquest by Thorfin, leader of the Viking colonists, who, with one hundred and fifty-one companions, fought off the Indians. This interpretation required imagination and patience, since the Roman numerals on the stone read 131 . . . which Rafn declared meant 151 in runic symbols.

The Dighton carvings have been stretched to cover so many different interpretations that it would have been more fitting had they been engraved on rubber. From the Biblical version to the Norse interpretations was quite a spread, equalled only by a remarkable performance from the Algonquin Indian sage Chingwauk. When he was asked by historian Henry Schoolcraft to interpret these Dighton carvings, Chingwauk promptly came up with a lengthy report alleging that the carvings described a great battle between two Indian nations, a conclusion even more fanciful than its predecessors.

181

Latest entry in the Dighton Rock Derby is the study made by Professor E. B. Delabarre of Brown University. After systematically demolishing the preceding interpretations, Professor Delabarre says that the carving tells the story of Miguel Cortereal . . . "by the will of God the leader of Indians."

And he may be right . . . for Miguel Cortereal reached Newfoundland in 1502 . . . nine years before the date of the Dighton carvings. Cortereal never returned to Portugal. The laborious carvings on the rock may tell his story, after four centuries, to those who can decipher it.

As Professor Delabarre admitted, "There is much that is debatable in the carving of Dighton Rock . . . it just depends on how you look at it."

45

Napoleon's Strange Death

Modern medical science is still seeking clues to a puzzle that has baffled historians for more than a century . . . the riddle of Napoleon's death.

In the village of Baleycourt, on the Meuse River in France, a faded page of the town records may hold part of the key to the strange death of Napoleon Bonaparte. On that page is inscribed the name of Francois Eugene Robeaud, "born in this village 1771 . . . died on St. Helena. . . ." The date of his alleged death on that sandy sunbaked island is illegible . . . obliterated long ago . . . and perhaps with good reason; for, in view of the existing evidence, it is not improbable that he died on St. Helena on May 5, 1821, under the name of Napoleon Bonaparte, whom he so closely resembled.

Bonaparte took great pains to secure doubles for himself, four of them in all, and one of that number was Francois Robeaud. One double died of poison just prior to Waterloo; another was crippled in a riding accident; still another was killed by a stray bullet; and only Robeaud was left when Napoleon's fortunes collapsed. He went back to live with his homely spinster sister in their cottage at Baleycourt.

Napoleon was banished to St. Helena, off the coast of Africa. The British and French were agreed that he must not escape again, as he had done from Elba. The French guarded him on the island itself, while the British furnished vessels to patrol the waters around the island.

Napoleon had friends, he had money, and he had patience. Working together, quietly, they could constitute the forces that would free him. Now see what happened.

In 1818 the French General Gourgard resigned his post of command at St. Helena, and was replaced by General Bertrand. Gourgard returned to Paris, presumably in retirement. About two months after Gourgard reached Paris, a fine coach arrived in Baleycourt. The coachman inquired the way to the home of Francois Robeaud. Who was in the coach, and why they were seeking Napoleon's double was never explained. Robeaud and his sister went about their customary routines for another month. The coach? Oh, just a physician who wanted to buy some rabbits for a friend. Nothing, really!

Both Robeaud and his sister vanished one night in the autumn of 1818, and neither was ever seen again in Baleycourt. The sister was later found living very comfortably in Tours, where she claimed that a physician was paying her bills, a purely platonic arrangement handled entirely by mail; in fact, by courier. And what of her brother . . . ? She explained that Francois had gone away to sea, but had failed to tell her where or how or when. Very close-mouthed fellow, you see.

To escape from St. Helena, Napoleon needed four things . . . a double, a ship, some friends, and some money. Now, he had all of them.

In the winter of 1818, about a month after Robeaud's

disappearance, General Bertrand's wife wrote to a friend, "Success is ours! Napoleon has left the island!"

In those same closing days of 1818, a well-dressed stranger who called himself Revard, came to the city of Verona, Italy. A merchant from the north of France, he said—a widower who wanted to open a small business; in his case, that of an optician who dealt in diamonds. He acquired a partner, Mr. Petrucci, who actually ran the business and who jokingly referred to Revard as the Emperor, because of Revard's remarkable resemblance to Napoleon.

According to subsequent sworn testimony of Petrucci and others, Revard received a courier on the afternoon of August 23, 1823. After reading the sealed message which was handed to him, he seemed greatly disturbed. He told Petrucci that he had to leave on a most important mission; and two hours later, as he got into the coach, he gave Petrucci a sealed letter with instructions to deliver it to the King of France if he, Revard, failed to return within three months.

Twelve nights later, shortly after eleven o'clock on September 4, 1823, lights were blazing brightly in Schonbrunn castle in Austria, where the son of Napoleon was critically ill with scarlet fever. A guard heard a rustling in the vines; he saw a shadowy figure drop to earth and run toward the castle. The guard fired—the intruder fell dying—shot through the abdomen.

The Captain of the guards took one look at the body and called the Colonel. Eventually the French Embassy took charge—until Napoleon's wife demanded that the stranger be buried in her own family plot, as was done.

Revard never returned to Verona. Petrucci delivered

the sealed letter to the King of France, and was paid handsomely for his service—and his silence. On Helena, death came at last to the prisoner known as Napoleon—a man who did not write like Napoleon—nor did he talk like Napoleon.

In 1821—the man on St. Helena died of cancer of the stomach. But in 1956 the British government revealed that they have in their possession a section of Napoleon's intestines. And that specimen shows clearly that its owner had died—not of cancer, as the man on St. Helena—but from a bullet wound . . . as the stranger in the garden of Schonbrunn castle!

46

John Keely's Mystery Motor

The powerful engine shook the building . . . but it shook the existing understanding of energy even harder.

Twenty-three men were crowded into the same small room which housed the controversial motor. Many of them were engineers, others were professional men or bankers—and all of them were investors. They were skeptics, too; and they had waited years for John Keely to make good on his claims. Time after time they had poured their money into his endless research and profitless development of the engine that now stood before them. Today he had promised them that he would show what it could do. Was he fraud or genius? They should soon know.

John Keely never even glanced at the hard faces of the men who were packed into the room with him and his engine. If he was aware of their presence he gave no hint —just as he apparently ignored the ear-shattering noise that was rattling the small window panes. From the heavy steel machine, bolted to the massive stone base, came the screech of metal in travail. A deep hum changed to a moan—the moan to a whine. Wilder danced the window frames—as though they were eager to flee this unearthly din.

Keely knew he was master of the situation, because he, and he alone, was master of the machine before them. These irate investors were demanding proof that their money had gone into something practical? Very well—they would soon have their proof! He lightly tapped a button, and the roar jarred the bones of every man present.

When the faint blue fog cleared away, the committee members could see that the one-inch lead ball had been expelled from the machine with such incredible force that it had shot completely through two heavy oak planks and buried itself in a sandbox against the wall.

Most impressive, the committee agreed; but when could they expect to put this latent power to work in a fashion that would reimburse the stockholders?

For John Keely this session with the stockholders' committee in November 1879 was an old, old story. He gave them performance—they insisted on profits. Over and over again, as the stockholders came and went, he endured their criticism and calumny. Through the years of ambivalence that surged about him, John Keely never lost his temper. Neither did he lose his ability to find new financial backers to replace those who had given and gone.

For a mechanical inventive genius, John had an unusual background. Born in Philadelphia in 1827, he worked as a carpenter, a violinist, a magician who specialized in card tricks; and finally he trudged to the Rocky Mountains as a trapper. Badly wounded by an Indian arrow, he made his way back to Philadelphia and eventually recovered from the wound.

It was an age when the need for controllable power was great. Water power could not meet the demands of growing industry. Steam power was not the answer—there must be some new cheap source of energy that could be harnessed to turn the wheels of the mills and factories.

John Keely first attracted attention by announcing, in 1871, that he had tapped a great new source of energy—as he put it with exasperating vagueness—"a device which disintegrates the etheric force that controls the atomic constitution of matter." Some scientists challenged him, some ignored him—all were skeptical of him.

Keely claimed that his engine operated on "harmonic vibrations." His detractors promptly retorted that the motivating force was hot air, generated by Mr. Keely. Whatever it was, it had enough power to bend steel rails and to tear giant hawsers into shreds, a force beyond anything in common use at the time.

In December, 1882, the angry investors demanded a showdown . . . and got it. Keely agreed to reveal the secret of his mystery motor to any scientist the committee named. They selected Edward Bakel . . . who saw and was convinced. He reported to the unhappy investors that, while he did not understand all that he had seen, he understood enough to know that Keely had discovered all he had claimed.

Keely's luck ran out in 1888, and the stockholders had him sent to jail for ignoring a court order to reveal his secret. A wealthy widow financed him for the next ten years, to the end of his life in 1898. The stockholders wrecked his shop, finally came upon a huge steel ball which contained compressed air. There was nothing new about that; for Keely had often shown the sphere to interested parties, and its pipes were inadequate to have operated at the pressures indicated by the performance of the machine.

The secret of Keely's mystery motor died with him.

Scientists could never agree on how it had operated. The witnesses agreed on only one thing; the engine made a humming sound. The question remains: Were they hearing the birth pangs of a great discovery . . . or merely the persuasive hum of a humbug?

47

The Treasure In The Well

Electronic instruments tell us there are tons of gold there—and it's yours for the taking; but getting it may take a bit of doing. . . .

If it's gold you want—real gold that is yours for the taking—then Oak Island may be the end of the rainbow for you. Like the proverbial pot of gold at the rainbow's end, you may find it a bit elusive—but on Oak Island it is there —no mistake about that! The lucky ones have touched some of it—the better-equipped seekers have watched the indicator needles on their electronic gear flutter to match their own hearts, but one and all they have had to admit defeat! For the treasure of Oak Island was so cunningly concealed that it has defied the best efforts of all comers for almost a century and a half.

Oak Island is a tiny rock knoll that sticks up from the cool blue waters of Mahone Bay, in Southern Nova Scotia. Nobody paid much attention to this insignificant speck of land until 1795. On a bright Sunday morning in April of that year three young men rowed out to the island . . . and spent the rest of their lives wishing they hadn't.

Tony Vaughn, Danny McGinnis, and Jack Smith knew

that Oak Island had been used as a haven of refuge and repair by the freebooters who infested the seas in those days. The pirates could anchor in one of the convenient deep coves on the north end of Oak Island, post a lookout in one of the several tall trees, and go about their business of removing the barnacles from the ships' bottoms in comparative safety.

Teach came there, according to local gossip, and Morgan and Steve Bonney, and other notorious scum of the seas. They came there and traded with the canny Nova Scotians, and they paid handsomely to the local authorities who looked the other way while the pirates camped out on Oak Island.

One by one the pirates had been hanged or driven from the seas, and when Smith, Vaughn, and McGinnis rowed over to the island in 1795 they knew that no pirates had been there, openly or otherwise, for at least seven years. But they knew too that the roistering freebooters had left a lot of evidence of their visits; pistols, knives, sometimes a gold coin or two could be scraped from the sand of the little beach where they gambled and fought and drank.

It was Tony Vaughn who called the attention of his companions to the worn place on the limb of the huge oak tree and to the depression in the soil directly beneath the same limb. They agreed that it looked very much like heavy ropes had been looped over the limb to lower something into a hole that had been later carefully filled in.

Working quietly in their spare time for several years, the boys dug down thirty-five feet. Then, in 1803, Smith told Dr. John Lynds of their strange find, and of the thick layers of coconut fibers they had discovered at the thirty-five-foot level. It was a fateful day for Dr. Lynds when he first stood there beside that pit; for in the ensuing years he spent his entire fortune probing its depths for the treasure he was so confident that it contained.

Workmen paid by the doctor pulled out, at successive ten-foot levels, layers of heavy oak planks, a layer of ship's putty, and more thick tough layers of coconut fiber, presumably hauled there by pirates who had loaded it in the West Indies, two thousand miles away. Beneath a layer of oaken planks at the eighty-foot level, the workmen found a flat stone covered with unintelligible hieroglyphics.

As a last resort, when his funds were virtually gone, Dr. Lynds brought in a large handpowered drill. With it he probed to a depth of a hundred feet from the surface. The drill cut its way through brittle plaster and more hardwood, then it seemed to drop into some sort of subterranean room. The next effort with the drill, racing against the water that was rising rapidly in the pit, brought up a few scraps of gold, and a bit of paper, and moments later . . . disaster. Water broke into the pit in such a rush that three workmen drowned.

Dr. Lynds was bankrupt.

If he had established nothing else, he had given his fortune and nine years of his life to show that there was gold in some sort of a man-made vault about one hundred feet below the scarred old oak tree.

It was forty-six years before Dr. Lynds was able to try again. In the gold rush madness of 1849, old and rheumy-eyed, he gathered about him a small group of financial backers. Their workmen reopened the crumbled pit, sank it ten feet deeper than ever before, until they came to a layer of cement. Their drill broke through into that room again . . . brought up a bit of gold chain . . . and again, just as success seemed inevitable, the water came pouring in and ruined them.

Other treasure seekers, including Franklin D. Roosevelt, have spent lavishly of their time and money there. They have confirmed that the gold is there, that it is cunningly protected by sea water brought in through ingenious tunnels . . . and that the gold is likely to stay there . . . for in 1957 the engineers found it as real . . . and as unattainable as ever.

48

Stories In Stone

Did the Vikings penetrate to Minnesota? Did they leave a graven record of their trip and its tragic finale? . . . What was the unusual inscription on the stone?

Historians are well aware that the Vikings reached the shores of the new world centuries before Columbus. There is ample evidence that they settled briefly as far south as Massachusetts. But did they also penetrate the St. Lawrence river and eventually enter the Great Lakes?

A farmer near Kensington, Minnesota, Olof Ohman, and his small son, Edward, dug up a slab of soft calcite on Ohman's farm in 1898 and were surprised, so they said, to discover that it was covered with some sort of inscription. For a while the stone remained little more than a local curiosity.

A few of the better-educated members of that predominantly Scandinavian community noted that the writing on the stone appeared to be similar to the old rune writing of their own ancestors.

Mr. Ohman sent the stone to Professor George Ohrme of Northwestern University, who examined it at length and informed the owner that it was spurious, a deliberate attempt by some unknown party to falsify history. Mr.

Ohman, a practical man, put the stone to use as a door-step for a feed bin.

Scholars are generally agreed that the inscription reads: "Eight Goths and 22 Norwegians on an exploring journey from Vinland very far west. We had camp by two skerries, one day's journey north from this stone. We were fishing one day when we returned home and found ten men red with blood and dead. A V M (Ava Virgin Mary) save us from this evil. We have ten men by the sea to look after our vessel forty-one (or fourteen) days' journey from this island. Year 1362."

The stone was purchased by Hjalmar Holand of Ephraim, Wisconsin, who then embarked upon a career of lecturing and writing on the subject; and his works converted a former skeptic, Professor Sigurdus Nordhal of the University of Iceland, to the belief that the story told by the stone is genuine.

Most other authorities on the subject are convinced that the carving on the soft calcite is of recent vintage, probably the work of two neighbors of Olaf Ohman, men who were known to have produced similar writings as practical jokes.

The weakness in the carving on the Kensington stone lies in the use of runic characters and expressions which were not a part of the language used by the 14th Century Vikings. Holand based his case largely on the record of a Viking expedition which left Norway in 1348 and did not return until 1364, plus the story of a small vessel which crept into the harbor of Straumfiord, Iceland, in 1347. If Holand is correct and the Kensington stone is indeed a record of Vikings in Minnesota in 1362, history would need some extensive re-writing.

196

From time to time these strangely inscribed stones crop up to plague the scholars. Such an incident occurred in the spring of 1937 in County Cork, Ireland, when a schoolboy cutting across fields on his way home picked up a stone to shy at a bird. The bird didn't move, so the lad searched about for another rock. He spied what appeared to be a small stone projecting from the sod . . . but as he attempted to pick it up it resisted . . . evidently it was larger and deeper than he had expected.

The lad kicked the stone, worked it loose and discovered that it was fully as large as his hand . . . and smooth on one side. Lo and behold! There was writing on the smooth side of the stone. Devil's writing, no doubt!—he dropped the stone and fairly flew across the fields to the little village where he lived . . . Straight to the home of the schoolmaster he went, and told his story. The schoolmaster laughed and told the boy not to worry . . . tomorrow they would have a look at it.

If the old teacher thought the boy was exaggerating, he had a surprise coming. There *was* writing on the stone, something that had been scratched into it a long time before. It had been buried so long that the age of the writing was going to be a matter for study by the experts, so the teacher took the stone to the University.

Then the fun began. One expert studied the markings for two months and said they were an ancient Hebrew warning of an invasion by sea. Another declared that they were unmistakably early Norse, telling of a hopeless fight against wild tribesmen after they had been shipwrecked on the nearby coast. Other experts read other interpretations into the same inscriptions.

It remained for an humble student to solve the mys-

197

tery. One day as he came into the classroom he glanced at the stone as it lay on a table in the late afternoon sun. At an acute angle, from the side, the message stood out clearly. It read: "June, 1788. Am very drunk again this day."

PART
THREE

49

The Invisible Fangs

Time after time, something sank its fangs into the screaming girl, even while police held her. But what it was, nobody knew. And nobody knows.

The night of May 10th, 1951, had been warm and quiet in Manila, until police brought that hysterical girl into headquarters.

The chief medical examiner slammed his hat on his head and snorted. "Nonsense!" he huffed. "Nonsense! You get me out of bed in the middle of the night to look at a girl who has epileptic fits!"

The Mayor of Manila said nothing. He looked in bewilderment from the irate doctor to the screaming girl. There were the welts on her arm, the teeth marks. Had she really inflicted them herself while in the throes of an epileptic seizure, or had they been savagely driven into her flesh, as she claimed, by something . . . or somebody . . . who had attacked her in her locked cell?

Mayor Arsenio Lacson did not know, but the case was so strange that the Chief of Police had been called and he in turn had called the Medical Examiner. Together they had gone to the jail to examine the cause of all the excitement—eighteen-year-old Clarita Villaneuva—just another of the countless homeless youngsters the war had left adrift in the streets of Manila. When police found her she was the center of a small crowd on a street corner, screaming that she was being attacked and bitten. The onlookers, most of them scum from the nearby taverns, were cheering her on and winking knowingly at each other, making signs to indicate that the girl was insane.

Dope, perhaps? Or absinthe? Whatever it was police left to others to determine. They seized the struggling girl and took her to a cell.

Clarita fell sobbing to the floor as the door clanged behind her. The police ignored her pleas to look at the eight sets of teeth marks where she said the Thing had bitten her.

The Thing? What thing? Clarita could only describe it as a thing that looked like a man, except that he had big, bulging eyes and was wearing a loose black cape, and he seemed to float in the air when he desired.

Just then she began to scream again, shrieking that the Thing was coming again, right thru the bars.

The exasperated policeman unlocked the cell door and led the girl into the hall, screaming at the top of her voice. And before his eyes, more teeth marks appeared on her upper arms and shoulders . . . livid marks surrounded by what appeared to be saliva. The officer ran for his Captain . . . and the Captain called the Chief.

After the medical examiner had gone home, the Mayor and the Chief of Police examined the marks on the girl for themselves. Self inflicted? Ridiculous, they told each other; no one could bite himself on the back of the neck, or on the back of the shoulders where this girl was bitten. Something strange here, indeed!

202

Clarita Villaneuva spent the rest of the night on a bench in the front office of the Manila police station, where she finally sobbed herself to sleep.

Next morning, as the police prepared to take her into court to face vagrancy charges, the girl began screaming again. The Thing was back, biting her! Two strong policemen grabbed her, one holding each hand, and before their astounded eyes and those of the reporters and the Medical Examiner himself, the teeth marks sank deep into her arms, the palms of her hands, and her neck. This attack lasted for at least five minutes until the girl fainted and sank to the floor. Medical Examiner Mariana Lara examined her again—and reversed himself. This girl was *not* having an epileptic seizure at all. The bites were real, but *not* self inflicted. He asked that the Mayor be called at once, and the Archbishop.

It was some thirty minutes before the Mayor arrived and by that time Clarita had regained consciousness. The bites on her arms were badly swollen and the palm of one hand was thick and bruised where the teeth prints had been deeply embedded. As the Mayor and the Medical Examiner accompanied her to the prison hospital, Clarita began shrieking that the Thing was after her again; and this time he had a helper, another bug-eyed creature. Mayor Lacson later testified that, as he watched, livid teeth marks appeared on opposite sides of her throat, on her index finger, and one set of teeth prints was deeply indented on the girl's hand even while the Mayor held it.

The fifteen-minute trip to the prison hospital was a nightmare for the Mayor of Manila, the medical examiner, the girl and the driver of the automobile. But once there, the attacks ceased and Clarita began her slow recovery.

She never again underwent such an experience. Said Mayor Lancon, "This is something that defies explanation." Said Medical Examiner Dr. Mariana Lara, "I was just scared stiff!"

50

None Came Back

What of the steamboat that sailed around the bend to oblivion in broad daylight? . . . or the army that marched down the road and vanished without a trace . . . where did they go?

The last stevedore had shuffled across the long gangplank to the river bank . . . the cargo of cotton and molasses was all aboard. Two long blasts on her mighty steam trumpet to warn small boats out of the way, and the Iron Mountain belched fire and smoke as she shoved off from Vicksburg that bright June morning in 1872. Moments later she had gone around the bend, pulling a line of barges, bound for Louisville with four hundred bales of cotton . . . then Cincinnati and finally Pittsburgh.

What happened to her after she vanished from sight around the bend in the river will probably never be known. But whatever her fate, it came swiftly and (let us hope) . . . mercifully.

The first inkling that something had gone wrong came a couple of hours later when another stern wheeler, the Iroquois Chief, had to churn the river with full emergency power to get out of the way of a string of runaway barges. Such things happened occasionally when tow lines broke, so the Iroquois Chief observed the customary amenities . . . it chased the barges and overtook them . . . and stood by to await the return of the Iron Mountain.

While they waited, the crewmen on the Iroquois noticed a peculiar thing. The tow rope on the barges had *not* broken. It had been *cut* . . . cleanly . . . a move that was taken only in emergencies when a steamboat was fighting for its life.

But the Iron Mountain was never seen again. If it had burned it would have been seen by other passing craft. If it had been snagged and sunk, the barrels of molasses and the cotton bales stacked on the deck would have littered the river for miles; and, if the boilers had torn it asunder, the evidence would have been unmistakable.

Instead, there was nothing.

The Iron Mountain, a brute of a river boat, 180 feet long, 35 feet wide took her cargo and her 55 passengers and crew around the bend to oblivion . . . without a trace.

On the morning of December 14, 1928, the Danish training ship Kobenhaven was preparing to leave the harbor at Montevideo. She awaited only the arrival of the fifty cadets who were taking part in a ceremony at the Danish consulate. It was to be their last cruise on a training vessel. When they got back to Denmark they would be enrolled as full fledged seamen. The future looked bright for the boys; but mercifully the truth was hidden from them,—for them the future consisted only of a few more hours.

Shortly before noon, the cadets came swinging aboard the Kobenhaven, singing as they marched down the gangplank. The ship steamed slowly out of the harbor, past a couple of small fishing vessels . . . and vanished. Incoming ships, which should have sighted her, saw neither the vessel nor any trace of her. The Kobenhaven, like the Iron Mountain before her, had sailed into oblivion.

History records several cases of vanishing armies, including four thousand trained and fully equipped troops who camped one night beside a small stream in the Pyrenees during the Spanish War of Succession. Next morning they had a rendezvous with destiny, for they broke camp . . . formed ranks and marched into the foothills—to disappear from the sight of their fellow men from that day to this.

It was a fate they shared with the 650 French colonial troops who were marching toward Saigon, Indo-China, in 1858. Trudging along the highway across open country only fifteen miles from the city, they vanished as completely as if they had walked off the earth.

Modern official military documents record the bare details of a mystery fully as baffling as those we have just mentioned. The Japanese sacked Nanking on December 10, 1939. Central China was a supine giant, helpless before the ravaging aggressors. It was imperative that the Japanese be delayed as long as possible, for every hour counted to the beleaguered Chinese forces. To this end, Colonel Li Fu Sien stationed his troops across an area in the rolling country south of Nanking.

Two hours later his aide reported that the troops did not respond to radio calls. Their guns were found stacked beside their little cooking fires, but the troops were gone. They could not have deserted across the open country without being detected. Japanese records reveal no trace of them as possible prisoners. And not one of the 2,988 missing men has ever been seen or heard from since that fateful day.

But if I were asked to cite one such case as strangest

of all, I would unhesitatingly refer to the twin-engine marine plane with thirty-two persons aboard which crashed on Tahoma Glacier, in 1947. Two days later searchers reached the plane. There was ample evidence that no one had survived the head-on crash; but what of the 32 men aboard the plane? A reward of five thousand dollars was offered for discovery of the bodies . . . but not one of them was ever found.

51

When Uncle Sam
Used Ghosts

The most notorious crime of the century was the Lindbergh kidnapping . . . when baffled authorities called in spiritualists . . . with surprising results.

The story began sometime in the early evening of March 1, 1932, when a fiend in human form committed the most widely publicized crime of the twentieth century.

He parked his car in a small clearing off the narrow gravel road that led through the heavily wooded countryside to the home of Col. Charles Lindbergh, a few miles from Hopewell, New Jersey. From the back seat of the car the kidnapper took a sectional ladder which he carried to the hedge that rimmed the Lindbergh lawn. There he assembled the ladder, carried it to the side of the house, and unerringly placed it beside the window of the room in which the twenty-month-old baby boy was sleeping. A few moments later, as he carried the child down the the ladder, it broke. Kidnapper and victim fell to the soft earth, which recorded the mishap for the police who came next day.

The hue and cry which followed the kidnapping of Charles Lindbergh, Junior, amounted to world-wide indignation. It brought into the news an assortment of unusual characters who contributed little to the case except delay.

There was a confused businessman from Norfolk, Virginia, who claimed that he had been contacted by the kidnappers; and days were wasted before the falsity of his claims became apparent.

There was a note from the kidnapper which led the authorities on a fruitless search for a boat on which the child was supposedly being held. The note was genuine, the boat was non-existent. Among the oddballs, there was the eccentric retired school teacher in the Bronx who placed an advertisement in a neighborhood paper which, by some improbable chance, happened to be the one paper the kidnapper read!

The ransom money was paid in gold certificates, a type of money subsequently withdrawn from circulation by the government. Eventually these bills led to the capture of a German war veteran named Bruno Hauptmann. He lived quietly with his wife and son in a modest home near the Bronx. Unemployed, he still had plenty of spending money, most of it the ransom money from the kidnapping. By entangling him tightly in a web of circumstantial evidence, the government led Hauptmann to the electric chair.

There were some strange angles to the case which were never explained. It is a matter of record that Hauptmann had at least two accomplices, a man and a woman; yet they were never found, and no effort was made to find them after he was captured. It is also a matter of record that part of the Lindbergh ransom money was never recovered, although Hauptmann had most of it. It was readily apparent that the kidnapper had known the movements of those inside the home the night the child was carried away—which may explain the suicide of Betty Gow, the baby's red-headed nurse.

At the height of the frantic search for the missing baby, when there was still hope that he would be found alive, the officers on the case were desperate. They were swarming around the Lindbergh home, waiting for some break—anything—that would help them solve the case.

The phone rang. It was a call from a man who identified himself as a Brooklyn minister. He told them that one of his parishioners had information concerning the case—information which could not be revealed until they were on the scene of the kidnapping.

Secret Service officers met the man and his companion at Hopewell next morning. He identified himself as a minister of a Spiritualist church, the woman with him, he explained, was a trance medium who would try to establish contact with the missing child if she could be placed in his room for an hour or so.

The annoyed Secret Service men could not take her to the Lindbergh home because of the highly disturbed condition of the expectant Mrs. Lindbergh; so they took her to the nearest house and to a room facing the same direction as that from which the baby had been abducted. The woman went into a deep trance; and for the next two and a half hours she told the two Secret Service men and a stenographer that the baby was in an unpainted house 4½ miles northeast of where they sat and that the kidnappers would kill the baby if searching parties approached, because they were watching the Lindbergh home through binoculars.

When the body of the Lindbergh baby was found on May 12, about three weeks after the weird seance, it was found about 4½ miles northeast of the Lindbergh home, a few hundred yards from an unpainted shack. The shack bore evidence that a baby had recently been there . . . and a red-haired woman . . . and that they had left hurriedly, as the medium had described.

Although the Secret Service had ignored the results of the seance, subsequent events showed that her statements had tallied closely with the facts—a set of circumstances which defies explanation by conventional science.

52

The Man With
The X-Ray Mind

When Scotland Yard came up against a blank wall time after time in its search for the missing Stone of Scone, it turned reluctantly to the one man who might be able to help: Peter Hurkos, the man with the X-ray mind.

The Stone had been stolen right out of Westminster Abbey in December, 1950, a crime that made headlines all over the world, and made laughing stock of the London police. Hurkos, a quiet, unassuming young Dutchman, met with the Scotland Yard representative in Dordrecht to discuss terms.

Together he and the detective flew to London where other officials and a police sergeant met him at the airport and rushed him to the scene of the sensational robbery. There, in the famed old Abbey, the authorities let him handle a tool abandoned by the thieves and a wrist watch lost by one of them. After hours of study of the scene and of the food scraps left by the thieves, Hurkos slowly traced on a map of the city of London the path which he said had been taken by the burglars as they hauled away the Stone.

213

Although he had never seen London before, he described in detail the buildings along the route he traced, and described the thieves, three men and a woman, in detail. When finally captured, three months later, they were found to tally with the descriptions Hurkos had given.

During the war, Peter Hurkos worked closely with the underground. When Dutch patriots became suspicious of a new member, they brought the man's picture to Hurkos. He ran his fingers over it for a few moments and said: "I see this man in the uniform of a German officer!" The man was subsequently watched closely, detected in the act of transmitting information to the Germans, and confessed to being an officer in the Nazi counter-espionage service—as Hurkos had predicted.

The police at Nijmegen, Holland, have good reason to be grateful to Hurkos. In August, 1951, the old Dutch city and the surrounding countryside were plagued with fires, unquestionably the work of one or more firebugs. More than two hundred armed men patrolled the area, but the fires continued to devour barns and houses and bridges. One night, several weeks after the rash of fires had begun, Hurkos was walking along with an old friend, a textile manufacturer of Nijmegen. Suddenly Hurkos stopped and told his friend that another fire would soon break out—this one at the farm of a family named Janson. Together the two friends hurried to warn the police, only to learn that the fire had been reported a few minutes before they reached the station.

The police were not only skeptical, they were rude; but Hurkos insisted that he could help them if given a chance. Shutting his eyes, he described the contents of the police captain's pockets, even to the partially obliterated brand name on a pencil stub. That did it! Hurkos got his chance, and the police of Nijmegen got their firebug.

First, Hurkos asked to be taken to the scene of several of the fires. Groping through the ashes, he finally came up with a charred screwdriver handle, felt it silently for a moment and said: "We must look for a boy—a boy in his teens." Shown the school yearbook pictures of every school-boy in town, Hurkos finally pointed to one in a group picture. "That one!" he said. "That is the one I want to talk to!"

He had named the 17-year-old son of one of the richest men in town. "Ridiculous!" the police captain snorted. But Hurkos kept right on talking: "In that boy's pockets you will find a box of matches in one pocket, a bottle of lighter fluid in the other—but this boy doesn't smoke."

Brought to the station, the boy denied everything, until Hurkos said: "Pull up the left leg of your overalls and show the police the scratches you got from the barbwire fence as you ran from the fire!" The scratches were there, and the boy broke down and confessed. He was sent to a mental institution.

The astounding solution made headlines, of course, but to Hurkos it was mere routine. Taken to the scene of a murder, where a man had been shot to death on his own doorstep, Hurkos rubbed the victim's coat for a moment and told police that the killer had been an older man with spectacles, a moustache, and a wooden leg—who had tossed the murder weapon to the roof of the house. They found the gun, and the fingerprints convicted the victim's father-in-law—who had a moustache, thick spectacles, and a wooden leg!

Peter Hurkos doesn't know how he arrives at the answers,

but in 1958 he was brought to the United States to be studied by a group of mental specialists. They, too, had to admit they were baffled by Peter Hurkos—the man with the radar brain—whose gift (whatever it is!) is indeed Stranger Than Science.

53

Strange Legacies

Many and varied are the last requests of men and women who set down instructions for the disposal of their estates. Since they are written by all sorts of people under all sorts of circumstances, it is small wonder that the law is forced to deal with some very strange legacies.

Some of the oldest wills on record date back two thousand years or more and were, almost without exception, documents intended to prevent bloodshed among the heirs of the persons who made the wills. Aristotle's will, written in 322 B. C., was scholarly, of course. He appointed friends as executors, named a proper guardian for his daughter, freed his female slaves and included directions for his burial.

The American Revolutionary War statesman, Gouverneur Morris, was a generous man who willed half of his sizeable fortune to his widow, with the provision that she should receive the entire fortune if she married again. But Patrick Henry, the oft-quoted firebrand legislator, did not share Mr. Morris' views. Henry ruled that his widow should have his estate only in case she remained single, otherwise she should receive nothing. He explained his views to a friend by saying: "It would make me unhappy to feel that

I have worked all my life only to support another man's wife!"

The will of Edgar Bergen gives evidence of his sentimental attachment for dummy Charlie McCarthy. Bergen bequeaths ten thousand dollars to the Actors' Fund of America, with the provision that the directors of that organization keep Charlie in good and serviceable condition. At least five hundred dollars of the bequest is to be used each year to entertain children in orphanages, hospitals, and other institutions; functions at which Charlie McCarthy is to be one of the featured performers.

Louis Pasteur, the famed French bacteriologist, left a will that was typical of this gentle man. He wrote: "This is my testament. I leave to my wife all that the law permits a man to leave. May my children never be able to stray away from the track of duty and keep always for their mother the tenderness that she deserves."

In 1934 a bottle was picked up on the shores of South Africa by a couple of prospectors who found it buried in the sands of the beach. The bottle contained a piece of parchment signed by one Felipe Segrandez, who identified himself as a castaway on an island somewhere near the equator and west of Africa. He told how he and five others from his ship, the Santa Cecille, had reached the island after their vessel had been demolished in a storm. All his companions were dead, he wrote, and he felt that his own time was short, so he laboriously penned in his own blood instructions for dividing his estate in Lisbon among his relatives. The missive was forwarded to Spanish authorities in Lisbon, but it was unlikely that they were able to carry out the instructions, since the will had been placed in the bottle 178 years before.

218

Women, too, make wills. One Bridget Fillison of Bournemouth left a will in 1938 in which she divided her estate between her sister and her husband. Bridget wrote that the sister was to deliver the husband's portion of the estate in person—"by taking it to the nearest pub where he will be found drinking to my absence."

Wills ofttimes must be written in haste and under most unusual circumstances, as for instance the case of the Wyoming rancher who vanished on an automobile trip through the mountains. When his car was found twenty-one days later, his body was pinned in the wreckage at the bottom of a canyon. He had lived five days in that predicament; and realizing that he was not likely to survive, he had taken his car keys and scratched out a brief will on the dashboard of the car . . . a document which the court accepted as legal.

George Washington, a very methodical man, left a will that covered twenty-five pages of foolscap. It named his wife and six other persons as executors and Washington explained that with seven persons on the list there would surely be some one of them to carry out all the provisions—and he was right.

Robert Louis Stevenson bequeathed his birthday to a friend who complained that her own fell on Christmas Day. P. T. Barnum had his will printed into a fifty-five page pamphlet which provided detailed instructions for distributing his fortune and for the maintenance of his circus and his beloved freaks, many of whom could not care for themselves.

The Frenchman, Rabelais, said in his will: "I have nothing. I owe much. All the rest I give to the poor."

Francis R. Lord of Sydney, Australia, left to his widow

one shilling—"for tram fare so she can go somewhere and drown herself."

Perhaps the strangest of all was the last will and testament of a wealthy, eccentric woman who lived in Cherokee County, North Carolina. She willed her estate to God. The court issued a summons and the sheriff went through the motions of trying to serve it. His report, filed in court, says: "After due and diligent search, God cannot be found in Cherokee County."

54

Numbers On
The Brain

His name was Tom Fuller. He was illiterate, a seventy-year-old slave—but he had the ability to outperform such modern marvels as Univac.

Old Tom had been born in Africa, captured by slave traders and sold into bondage in Virginia. Until he was seventy years old there was little reason to regard him as anything more than a run-of-the-mill slave.

Tom was standing in a fence corner of his master's Virginia plantation one hot afternoon in August of 1779, waiting for the overseer to assign him to another task. He was just one of a little group of seven ragged slaves who stood patiently and quietly while the overseer and the owner of the plantation fumbled with a problem in arithmetic.

How much was the crop on that farm worth at current tobacco prices? The owner came up with one answer, the overseer arrived at another. Both were obstinate men and both were poor hands at simple arithmetic. They figured. They argued. Tempers were beginning to flare when the owner threw down his pencil and paper with a curse.

Old Tom removed his floppy felt hat and stepped forward.

"Please, Massa," he said. "I can tell you the answer to that figgerin', suh!"

The surprised owner invited Tom to give him the answer—if he could—and Tom promptly provided a figure which later proved to be correct. It also proved that both the plantation owner and the overseer had been wrong in their calculations. A schoolteacher who confirmed Tom's solution went to the plantation to put the illiterate slave to the test, and came away more mystified than ever, for old Tom heard the problems and furnished the answers in a flash.

One of the problems, which the teacher had worked out in advance of the test, called for the old slave to reduce 70 years, 12 days and 12 hours to seconds. In 90 seconds Old Tom gave them his answer. The schoolteacher and the plantation owner shook their heads. Sorry, but the old slave's answer did not match their own. Later, when they rechecked their calculations they discovered that Tom's figure was the correct one; his examiners had failed to take into consideration the leap years involved, a mistake that Tom had not made.

Tom became a sensation and his proud owner refused many tempting offers to sell him to promoters who wished to exploit him. The owner permitted scholars to come and put Tom to the test and without exception they went away with the answers to their problems, but without answer to how this old slave functioned as a human calculating machine.

Another Negro whose strange powers baffled science was Charles Cansler of Knoxville. He was a member of the bar and was also principal of Austin, a Negro high school in Knoxville.

As late as 1915, Cansler was touring the country giving demonstrations of his remarkable abilities. He could carry in his mind figures involving many millions and could instantly give the squares of such figures, generally beating the best existing calculating machines by sizeable margins. One of his most effective exhibitions was that with which he customarily opened his performances. Heavily blindfolded and with his back to the blackboard, spectators would write long columns of figures on the board. Then Cansler would remove the blindfold, walk to the blackboard and instantly write the correct total of the figures on the board. In the three or four seconds required for him to cross the stage, his mind had computed the total. Cansler's high level of general intelligence was in marked contrast to the mental quality which characterized many of these human calculators.

Like Old Tom Fuller, Jedidiah Buxton was illiterate. Born in England in 1707, he had no schooling, but for unknown reason was always fascinated by numbers and in fact was unable to concentrate on anything else. As a child he mentally calculated the number of lentils in his soup; the grains of salt in a cellar of a given size. In church he sat quietly through the services but, when they were over, Jed Buxton could recall nothing except the number of words in the sermon. When he walked around a field, he could tell how many square inches it contained. Once, for his own amusement, he calculated how much a farthing would be worth if it were doubled 139 times. In pounds sterling the answer requires a 39 digit number. Buxton was asked to multiply this fantastic sum by itself. Two and a half months later he produced the correct answer, explaining that he had worked on it at intervals during that time. An oddity of Buxton's performance was that, once he started on a complicated problem, he could forget it and pursue his normal activities; as though his brain were some sort of machine that carried on its complex functions unassisted, once it began.

There have been many of these astounding cases, none of which is explainable by conventional science. They constitute a natural grant of extraordinary mental powers and they also constitute another well-documented mystery located in the no man's land of the human mind.

55

Exposing India's
Phoniest Mysteries

For centuries India has been noted for its fascinating enigmas, a land of magic and malarky. Some of its strangest stories, sad to say, don't stand up well under careful scrutiny. For example: —

Let's turn back the pages of history . . . to the year 1756 when the last of the native princes of India had risen in defiance of the British East India Company. It was a brave gesture, but a futile one. These thousands of untrained men, the native troops, flung themselves en masse against the guns and bayonets of the British troops. It was the old, old story of spears against rifles . . . a spectacle that was not to be repeated on such a scale until the Italians swept into Ethiopia almost two centuries later.

The British problem was to lure the natives into pitched battles where British guns could easily decide the issue. Time after time they were able to achieve this, and time after time the Indian troops retreated from the field after staggering losses. The superiority of the British guns was countered by the fanatical zeal of the natives—and by their apparently endless supply of manpower.

But not every battle ended in victory for the British. From time to time their opponents eluded them—or poured into the fighting in such numbers that the British had to retreat to avoid being overwhelmed.

So it was on the night of June 20, 1756, that a detachment of British troops became separated from their comrades in the ebb and flow of battle. They formed their lines around a little knoll, but the gathering darkness made their muskets useless. Elephants trumpeted and charged through them. They surrendered to the Nawab of Siraj.

The British stacked their arms and marched off to prison. Actually they were marching into the pages of history, making their entrance through a non-existent aperture called the Black Hole of Calcutta—an indestructible legend that has defied truth for almost two hundred years.

Since most historians merely copy from other historians, the legend of the Calcutta atrocity has lived on. The conventional story from the conventional history books says that 146 of those British troops were jammed into a room only 14 by 18 feet, where 123 of them died during the night, victims of suffocation.

Some historians go on to add the harrowing details . . . how the victims were packed together so tightly the dead could not fall to the floor . . how the dead and the living still stood together at daybreak. That was the infamous Black Hole of Calcutta, an atrocious fabrication that lives on in the pages of history, thanks to the plagiarism of the historians.

Careful research by both the British and Indian governments disclosed the falsity of the "Black Hole of Calcutta." It was, in fact, just another rumor spread to infuriate the British people, especially the troops. Further investigation revealed that most of the British prisoners who supposedly died in that hole actually lived to a ripe old age in England.

The whole fraudulent story had been concocted by a minor officer of the British Embassy some years after the alleged event. Correspondents quoted him, historians quoted them.

In 1900, a board of inquiry consisting of eminent scholars from seven nations presented to the British Governor of India irrefutable proof that the widely publicized "atrocity" at Calcutta was an outright lie, perpetrated by an irresponsible minor official as propaganda; and the "suffocated" victims had gone to England, as shown by the British Army records.

With typical British thoroughness, the Governor considered the evidence carefully and then gave his decision; on the spot where the atrocity never happened he poured a great slab of concrete, engraved with the lurid and fictitious details. It is as imperishable as the story in the history books . . . a memorial to a lie.

The Calcutta story is on a par with that of the wolf girl of Midnapore, first recorded for credulous Americans by Dr. Gesell, writing in Harper's Magazine in 1930. He says his investigation showed that a female wolf near Midnapore, India, had adopted a small human baby which had been left in the open to die. The animal took the infant to her den.

Being such an avid researcher, Dr. Gesell left no rug unturned. He tells us that in the wolf den there was no furniture, no books, no rugs, and no dishes, and that true table manners were completely lacking. Having enlightened us on the lack of culture in the wolf den, he goes on to say that the abandoned baby learned to eat by putting the food directly into her own mouth and chewing—a procedure which has since been adopted by infants in many lands. The child learned to run on all fours, he says, but was captured by Reverend J. L. Singh of Midnapore, where she lived until 1929, howling each night at ten.

Her death was only physical, for the story of Kamala, the wolf girl of Midnapore, goes marching on. It had been reprinted in the pages of Coronet, the Saturday Evening Post, Colliers, Scientific American, and others which have never bothered to check a few simple facts. They have all taken Dr. Gesell at his word.

Unfortunately for the story, the facts betray it. There were no wolves in that part of India; the child was not found among wolves but on an ant hill. That she slept curled up proves that she had a flexible backbone and nothing else. And Dr. Gesell hangs his story by stating that it happened in the tiger-infested jungles of northwest India. Actually, Midnapore is on the opposite side of India, only seventy miles from Calcutta.

Kamala, the wolf girl, was probably an abandoned child, none too bright; but at least smart enough not to write magazine articles without first locating the place on the map.

56

The Song That Wrote Itself

Abraham Lincoln called it the song that saved the Union, The lady who wrote it called it the song that wrote itself. Perhaps both were right.

The "Battle Hymn of the Republic" is one of the most stirring songs ever written. Abraham Lincoln cried the first time he heard it—during the darkest days of the Civil War. The music to "Battle Hymn" came from an old southern camp meeting song, "Say, brother, will you meet us on Canaan's happy shore?" But where the words came from was quite another story—and a very strange one.

On the night of November 18, 1861, the fog from the nearby Potomac River was drifting through the streets of the nation's capital. Long lines of dispirited Union soldiers shuffled past Willard's Hotel. Some of them stumbled along, for they had been marching all day; marching with heavy hearts from the defeats of yesterday to the uncertainties of tomorrow.

In a corner room of Willard's famed hotel, the pretty red-haired wife of a Boston social leader sat beside her window in the darkened room, watching the long lines of troops trudging past in the gloom. Ordinarily Julia Ward

Howe would have been asleep at this hour, but this was no ordinary occasion. Fate had chosen her for a strange mission.

"I have seen him in the watchfires of a hundred circling camps—"

The campfires from the Anacostia flats blinked at her through the mists over the Potomac—

"I have read a fiery gospel writ in rows of burnished steel—"

The yellow rays from the gaslight on the corner gleamed fitfully on the gunbarrels and bayonets of the marching troops.

Mrs. Howe watched the living panorama for a long time before she decided to retire. She was exhausted from her long train ride from Boston, and she slept soundly.

Shortly before daylight, she found herself sitting at the writing desk in the corner of the room. She wrote rapidly, which was unusual for her. Heretofore she had always found rhyming difficult, but on this cold gray dawn her pen flew across the paper, scratching out the lines that were to make her name live in history. It was so dark in the room that she could scarcely see the paper, but she did not bother to light the candle on the desk. She wrote as one inspired. If this was her mission in life, she was fulfilling it magnificently.

Long after daylight, when she awakened, she found that she had written a poem of five verses on a sheet of stationery from the Sanitary Commission, a government agency where her husband worked. She recalled vaguely sitting at the desk, but remembered nothing of what she had written. Yet there it was, so well written that she felt compelled to change only four words in the entire work.

It was entitled "The Battle Hymn of the Republic," but she could recall neither the verses nor the title.

What to do with this moving piece of work? She mailed it to the Atlantic Monthly, where it was published as a poem in the February issue of 1862. They sent her a check for four dollars.

Great songs, like great men and great ideas, must arrive on the scene at exactly the right time and place—and so it was with the masterpiece of Julia Ward Howe.

Her forceful and moving little poem fell into the hands of Chaplain Charles McCabe of the 112th Ohio volunteers, who had it in his pocket when he was captured at Winchester and sent to Libby prison. McCabe noticed that Mrs. Howe's poem fitted perfectly to the tune of John Brown's Body, which had been borrowed from the old southern song "On Canaan's Happy Shore." McCabe sang "Battle Hymn" to his fellow prisoners, and they soon sang it with him. One night, when a Confederate guard told the prisoners that the rebels had just won another smashing victory in Pennsylvania, the prisoners were sunk in gloom. But a few minutes later, another trusty, who served in the officers' mess at the prison, brought them the real story . . . that the Union had won a great victory at a little town called Gettysburg. McCabe and his fellow prisoners sang the "Battle Hymn of the Republic" till the windows rattled. . . .

"His truth goes marching on—"

Months later McCabe was released as an exchange prisoner and sent back to Washington. There, in a theatre, he told the audience of his experiences in Libby prison, and of the song that shook the walls. He sang it for them . . . and suddenly they were singing it with him. President

Lincoln rose to his feet, tears streaming down his cheeks, and asked them to sing it again.

Julia Ward Howe said of her masterpiece, "I wonder if I really wrote it. I feel that I did not. . . . I was just an instrument. . . . It really wrote itself!"

When she died in 1910 at the age of 91, a chorus of one hundred little children from the Perkins Institute for the Blind told her goodbye as they softly sang—

"With a glory in his bosom that transfigures you and me. . . ."

57

Did The Victim
Solve Her Murder?

The police were desperate after weeks of investigation had failed to solve the disappearance of Joy Aken. Did she tell them where to find her killer? Police records say that she did.

Science is admittedly operating under difficulties when it endeavors to explore the mind. The very nature of the study precludes success in many respects. Science has learned a great deal about the mind in the past three decades, thanks to new instruments and new techniques; but, reduced to its fundamentals, it becomes a program of the *mind* studying the *mind,* and that complicates the problem. We know that the human mind is capable of some remarkable feats which we can only record without understanding. That it may also be capable of other and even more incredible attainments is a matter for debate.

For example—let us examine the case of Joy Aken, found in the police records of Pinetown, Natal, South Africa, under the date of October 9, 1956, attested by four police officials and forty-six invited witnesses.

Joy Aken was a few days past seventeen when she vanished in mid-September, 1956. She was a very pretty girl, and she was also very shy. Joy had no steady boy friend,

233

and she had no enemies. Why, then, had she disappeared?

Her family suspected foul play, and the police concurred. They sent out bulletins bearing her picture to police posts throughout South Africa. A reward was offered for anyone who could provide information leading to the finding of the girl—or her body.

Weeks passed without results. There were a few crank tips—the usual crackpot reports which are to be expected—and as usual they came to naught. Joy Aken had vanished as completely as if the earth had swallowed her . . . which police suspected was literally true.

The missing girl's brother, Colin Aken, visited the police station in Pinetown each day in the hope that they might have learned something that would lead them to the end of their search, whatever that might be. Each day they had to tell him that they had found nothing; and by October 8 they admitted utter defeat.

That day, Colin heard, through a friend, of a retired headmaster of a school, Nelson Palmer, who had located missing items for some of his close personal friends. Mr. Palmer did this, said the friend, by relaxing, closing his eyes and describing what his mind seemed to see. He was embarrassed by the knowledge that he could do this and never discussed it for fear of ridicule.

Colin Aken and the Pinetown office of the South Africa Police were of the same opinion; they had nothing to lose by asking Mr. Palmer to try. A senior police officer visited Palmer and his wife that night, and finally secured their consent to a meeting on the following day, October 9, 1956.

While fifty persons sat silently in the two front rooms and hall of Mr. Palmer's home, he leaned back in his chair and closed his eyes. His breathing became heavy and labored. Sweat covered his face and began to trickle down from his chin. For minutes there was only the sound of his breathing; and many who were present began to suspect that that was going to be the extent of the program. Then Palmer's lips began to move; but the sound that came from them was a voice like that of a young girl—a young girl in terror.

"I am dead . . ." said the voice. Then there was a silence for two minutes, according to the police account . . . after that Palmer's lips began moving again, "My body is in the ravine near the High Rocks . . . a man has attacked me . . . he is killing me." Palmer's eyes opened and he seemed to be staring without seeing. A few minutes later he began breathing normally and arose from the chair.

Says the record: "Mr. Palmer then told us that the girl's body was partially concealed under some stones near a culvert at a spot about sixty miles from Pinetown. The murderer, he said, was a man named Clarence, about thirty years old, who had hidden the murder weapon, whatever it was, in an outbuilding at his home. Mr. Palmer said he believed he could lead us to the place where the body was hidden."

One hour and forty minutes later, Palmer led police to a lonely spot on the highway along the Natal coast. There, under a culvert and partially hidden by stones, they found the body of the missing girl. Joy Aken had been beaten and shot to death.

What of the killer? Palmer had described him as a man named Clarence. Relatives recalled that Joy had known a chap by that name—Clarence Gordon VanBuren. Ten hours later, police placed VanBuren under arrest. In a shed behind his home they found a gun which he later identified as the murder weapon. It was the old, old story of a frustrated lover. He had lured her into his car—lost his temper, struck her, then shot her to death in a fit of anger.

How did Palmer know where to find the body? Joy's family prefers to think the dead girl told him . . . somehow. Palmer scoffs at the idea. Nothing supernatural about it, he says, and he adds—"I have found missing pieces of jewelry by the same process; and they certainly don't tell me where they are. I think the human mind has some perfectly normal capabilities which we do not understand, and this projection in time is one of them."

58

Radar Tackles
A Monster

Prior to 1932, Loch Ness was just another of the beautiful lakes that help to make Scotland such an unforgettable place. But on November 12, 1932, the era of serenity came to an end.

Hugh Gray, a businessman of Foyers, was taking a walk around the lovely lake, as he had done so many times before. He was about midway between Dores and Port Augustus, and he stopped to fill his pipe. Hugh was on the northeast side of the point, where he had a good view of that portion of the lake.

Suddenly the water boiled up, a couple of hundred feet from shore. A great, black brute of a body welled up from the depths, forty feet or so of something gigantic and powerful, Hugh later reported. It threshed about in the water, occasionally waving a thick pointed tail, as though it were struggling with something that kept its head beneath the surface.

Hugh swung his old view camera around and managed to take five snapshots before the thing sank beneath the waves and the turbulence subsided. In all his years around the lake, Hugh had never seen anything remotely like it. He hurried home and developed the films. They didn't show anything distinctly, but they did show enough to substantiate his report that something exceptionally big and powerful had created a disturbance where he had seen it.

Old timers around the lake were least surprised by Hugh's report. The oldsters had seen it, too, they said, but they had kept quiet because nobody would have believed them. If the monster were really there, it had been there a long, long time . . . or perhaps there were more than one—if there were any.

Just about six months after Mr. Gray snapped his picture, a group of wealthy London hunters came to the lake as the guests of a surgeon who had leased some area for wild fowl shooting along the north shore. Several of these men reported that they watched in astonishment as a great, knobby, dark-gray body slowly rose to the surface near them, finally projecting a long, snaky-looking neck and a small head several feet out of the water. What's more, they got two pictures of the thing. Not really good pictures, for the surgeon who was handling the camera was admittedly somewhat shaken by what he was witnessing. The pictures corroborated the reports of the duck hunters, and their subsequent publication in a London newspaper fanned the controversy to white heat again.

The Loch Ness "monster" was a topic that divided the public into two distinct categories: Those who regarded the whole thing as a hoax—and those who stoutly defended the witnesses and accepted the existence of the thing as an unquestionable verity.

Naturally, numerous "experts" of all sorts rushed into print. They dismissed the Loch Ness monster by such varied explanations as a seal, a sea lion, a crocodile, a white whale, a sturgeon, a catfish, a tortoise, and a rotting tree trunk. Each expert had his moment in the spotlight before he was elbowed aside to make room for the next guesser. Meanwhile, plans were formulated for a quiet but systematic study of the lake itself, a landlocked body of water that ranged down to seven hundred feet in depth; a body of water darkened by the seepage from the peat bogs; cold water, unfished except for hardy souls who used hand lines near the surface. It was unfished, not well charted, but worthy of study in view of the conflicting claims.

Sir Edward Mountain arranged for twenty watchers with binoculars to scan the lake each day, beginning in July of 1934. Their reports developed rather regular appearances of the monster, to such an extent that Sir Edward got some movies of the thing a few weeks later.

The enigma was seen again from time to time, but it was October of 1954 when a bus driver stopped so that his passengers could watch the monster playing around on the surface for a full ten minutes; not more than a hundred yards away—a dark gray, long-necked, knobby looking brute, just as Hugh Gray had seen it so many years before.

In December of 1954, the fishing trawler, Rival, was crossing the lake on her way to drop her nets on the west side when the electronic echo-sounder suddenly began to chart an unusual object beneath the boat.

This underwater radar drew a picture of something swimming at a depth of five hundred and forty feet, about two-thirds of the way to the lake bottom. The thing had a small head on a long neck, eight short legs, a tail about fifteen feet long, and the object was about fifty feet from tip to tail. Experts who examined the chart said that it had recorded some living creature—that radar had proved the existence of a monster in Loch Ness—after all these years!

59

Billionaire Beggar

From a ragged urchin sleeping in the gutters, to one of the richest men in the world is quite an improvement . . . but one man made it . . . thanks to a cobra!

There were few travelers on that dusty road in India. The heat was stifling. Bandits were numerous. The ruler, called the Gaekwar, was a sort of feudal baron whose minions exacted tribute from all who used the road. Travel was dangerous and expensive, so only the brave or the beggars shuffled through the heat.

Shortly after noon, when the ruler's toll takers were dozing at their posts, a dirty, ragged boy stumbled up to the little well and furtively snatched a drink of water. His eye fell on a scrap of food beside one of the sleeping guards, hardly a bite, but the boy grabbed it from the dirt and ate it. Then he shuffled off down the road a few hundred yards until he came to a little clearing beside the path. A house had burned to the ground there; but that had been years before, and the weeds had long since covered the charred remains. The boy stretched out on the grass in full view of the road. He had nothing to lose and, therefore, nothing to fear. In a matter of moments he was sleeping the deep sleep of utter exhaustion.

He had an appointment with destiny. That boy went to sleep a beggar, and awoke to find himself rich and famous.

The time was the mid-1870's. A Maharajah had tried to poison an agent of the famed East India Company. The Maharajah was too powerful and dangerous to be executed, yet the incident could not go unpunished. The British deposed the Maharajah for what they called misconduct, a magnificent understatement. And since the deposed bigwig had no son to succeed him, an immediate search was instituted to provide a suitable successor. The dowager Maharanee sent out agents to scour the countryside.

Thus, on that sunbaked afternoon as the countryside lay gasping for breath, the tired and frustrated agents of the Maharanee were trudging along the road at a time when all other travelers were seeking the shade.

The agents walked along in silence. They came at last to the bend in the road where the house had burned down. One of the agents gasped and stopped in his tracks, clutching the sleeve of his companion.

In the clearing a few yards from the road lay a ragged boy, sleeping soundly. And beside him, reared so that its shadow fell across the lad, was a huge and deadly cobra! That snake was shading the face of the sleeping boy with its outspread hood; and was it not written that any man above whom the cobra raises its hood is destined to rule? The agents were jubilant, for their long and tiring search had come to a dramatic end. They squatted patiently in the shade of a nearby tree until the cobra went away; then they awakened the bewildered boy and apprised him of his good fortune.

241

By a superb exhibition of splitting hairs, the authorities discovered, so they said, that the beggar-boy's ancestors had been mountain kings of a long lost tribe. With that vague ancestry and with the more immediate blessing of the cobra's shadow, he became the official ruler of the state of Baroda.

Under the benign administration of this beggar, the people soon acquired a good education. When he became of age, he took over the reins of a state which had been notorious for its corruption and backwardness. The three million subjects were, in fact, little more than slaves.

Under the benign administration of this peasant boy turned prince, Baroda prospered and its people prospered, too. Almost singlehandedly the ruler broke the vicious caste system. He saw to it that every village had pure water, and at least one school and one doctor. He developed and installed a parliamentary form of government, including laws which banned polygamy and child marriage. Baroda became, by the turn of the century, an island of freedom and light in the sea of human misery known as India.

The Gaekwar had use for his ingenuity on his own behalf, too. He wanted to marry the lovely wife of a Hindu prince. Being a Hindu, she could not get a divorce, so she became a Mohammedan and got a divorce. As a Mohammedan, the Gaekwar could not marry her, so she became a Hindu again and the marriage was performed. Cupid had strained a point on behalf of this benevolent ruler, even though in reality he was just a beggar boy turned billionaire . . . thanks to the shadow of a snake!

60

The Dream Said
"Murder!"

A child killer was at large and the country was in an uproar, when a young man woke up screaming. Had he really, as he said, witnessed a murder while he was asleep?

The brutally ravaged body of five-year-old Dorothy Schneider had been found in the bushes alongside a country lane, where the fiend who killed her had tossed her aside with no attempt to conceal the crime. A witness had seen the child get into a robin's-egg-blue sedan. Beyond that there was nothing except the mute evidence borne by the child's body.

The countryside around Mount Morris, Michigan, was in a furor. The citizens had reason to be both alarmed and angered, for there was a monster in their midst. The corpse of an eighteen-year-old girl had been removed from the grave and dismembered. Several children, most of them little older than ill-fated Dorothy Schneider, had been accosted by a man who made it a practice to remain in the shadows where they could not get a good look at him. A midget, dressed as a child, was secretly brought in as bait for the monster, but the killer was too smart to be taken on such a ruse. Only once did pursuers get close, through a fluke, and little good it did them; for the fellow leaped nimbly over a fence, climbed a tree, jumped to a rooftop and vanished.

The body of little Dorothy Schneider was found on January 12, 1928. On the following night a group of outraged citizens met in the home of a local businessman for the purpose of forming a posse to hunt down the terrorist.

After a brief talk by a local law enforcement officer, who cautioned them about taking any hasty action, they heard from Deacon Adolph Hotelling who added his own warnings to those of the officer. Those present knew Hotelling as a fanatically devout man and they respected him. No one took offense when he, too, cautioned them against taking matters into their own hands. "Vengeance is mine saith the Lord," the Deacon reminded them, and he added, "We must ask God's help in times like this!" Suiting the action to the word, Deacon Hotelling dropped to his knees and prayed silently for several minutes, while his audience fidgeted nervously. Presently the Deacon arose. "Gentlemen," he said, "I have asked God to help us, and he has promised it to me."

There was an embarrassing silence. The Deacon bade the group good night and left. He had an appointment at his church, to rehearse a ceremony scheduled for the following Sunday. On that date Hotelling was elevated to an elder of the church, and a twenty-five-year-old carpenter, Harold Lothridge, was appointed to fill Hotelling's old office as deacon. The services were over at about ten-thirty.

A few minutes past two in the morning, Lothridge woke up screaming. His wife snapped on the bed lamp. Lothridge couldn't speak for a few moments; then he said, "I've

244

had a nightmare, a terrible thing! The most horrible experience of my life!"

"What about?" his wife demanded.

"That child! That little girl who was murdered near Mount Morris last week. I was somewhere near when the car drove up. I saw the man who killed her! I could hear the little girl crying—'I want to go home! I want to go home!' "

The incredulous wife urged him to go on. . . .

"Both of us know the killer very well," said the shaken young man. "It was Adolph Hotelling!"

Lothridge and his wife slept no more that night. He talked it over next day with his father, who warned him that his story was fantastic, and insupportable, and advised him to keep it to himself.

But the cat was already out of the bag; for two fellow workmen had overheard Lothridge's discussion with his father. That afternoon two deputy sheriffs came to talk to him, and Lothridge told them of his harrowing dream. They decided to squelch the story while they were about it, so they drove on over to Hotelling's house, where they found him at home.

The deputies asked him a few routine questions including whether he owned a robin's-egg-blue sedan. Hotelling smiled. "My car is black," he said. "But you are welcome to confirm for yourselves." He led them to his garage and, sure enough, the car was black. But, as one of the deputies turned to leave the garage, a big lodge ring on his finger scratched the car; and beneath the coat of black paint there was a layer of robin's-egg-blue!

Hotelling saw it too—and lost his composure. He broke down and confessed the whole gruesome story; the grave-robbing; the murder of Dorothy Schneider; and other outrages which had not yet been detected. He sobbed, "That little girl comes back to me every night. She keeps crying, 'I want to go home!' over and over again!"

Adolph Hotelling, the pious monster, was adjudged insane and sentenced to life imprisonment, trapped by the strange dream of Harold Lothridge, of which Lothridge says, "I have always felt that I was merely the instrument through which God gave us the help that Deacon Hotelling prayed for."

61

Who Planned The Murder Of Abraham Lincoln?

The five persons who were killed in connection with Lincoln's assassination were not alone in the plot. Was a member of Lincoln's own cabinet involved?

When the shocked nation recovered from the impact of Lincoln's murder, it cried for vengeance on the perpetrators of the infamy. Eventually four persons were hanged as conspirators in the plot, after a trial that was marked by callous disregard of any evidence that did not fit the preconceived sentence. And the vain, bombastic trigger man, John Wilkes Booth, died, according to the general understanding, as the result of being shot by a religious fanatic named Boston Corbett, although Corbett's claim is subject to question.

It is important to note that with Booth dead (killed before he could make any public statements—) and with the execution of the four co-conspirators from Booth's boarding house, any higher-ups who might have been involved were reasonably safe from exposure.

On the night of Lincoln's murder, Secretary of War Edwin M. Stanton hurried to the house where the President was dying and took charge of the investigation. For five hours Stanton refused to identify Booth as the killer. Booth was using those five hours to escape. And he left Washington over the only bridge which had not been closed by official order an hour before the murder.

Booth was surrounded in a barn by a contingent of troops under the command of Lieutenant Luther Baker, who had been assigned to this task by his uncle, Lafayette Baker, a slippery character who headed the Secret Service. The Secret Service was under the command of Secretary Stanton. Lafayette Baker was an intimate of Stanton; and Baker was detested by President Lincoln.

Sergeant Corbett, who was permitted to claim he shot Booth to death, was thirty feet from Booth when the assassin was paid off in his own coin. Only Lieutenant Baker was in the barn with Booth. Corbett was armed with a rifle. Booth was killed by a pistol bullet in the back of the neck, fired from such short range that Booth was powder-burned. Only one man could have fired that shot— Lt. Baker. Booth was silenced.

According to his own testimony, when Lafayette Baker told Stanton that Booth had been found, Stanton dropped into his chair and covered his face with his hands. When Baker added that Booth was dead, Baker says, Stanton dropped his hands and smiled for the first time in days.

At the trial, Stanton first testified that he did not have Booth's diary. Later, he was permitted to change his testimony to say that he did have the diary, but when he produced it in court, the twenty-four pages covering the critical period preceding Lincoln's murder were missing. Baker testified that the diary had been complete when he turned it over to Stanton. The military court made no effort to require Stanton, the Secretary of War, to explain his position and his contradictory testimony.

Part of the damning testimony which sent Mary Suratt and her three companions to the gallows came from a trio of dissolute characters whose veracity was the least of their virtues, if any.

One was Louis Weichmann, an employee of Mr. Stanton's own War Department, and a roomer at Mary Suratt's, where the crime was plotted. Weichmann talked about the plot openly for months before the murder, but no one in the War Department showed any interest in him, until his testimony was needed to convict! As long as Stanton remained in government service, Weichmann loafed on government jobs. After Stanton was ousted, Weichmann was discharged.

The tavern keeper, John Lloyd, who testified that Mary Suratt used him as a supply depot for the assassin, during his testimony quoted her at length, word for word, yet at the time of their talk he had admittedly been falling-down drunk.

John Parker was a man who had a police record himself when Mrs. Lincoln had him appointed White House guard in April of '63. It was John Parker who left his post in Ford's theatre, walked into a nearby bar where Booth was waiting, an indication to Booth that the way to the President was unguarded. Yet Parker was never prosecuted for his incredible dereliction to duty. It may be coincidence, but only as long as Stanton held power, Parker remained on the police force. Why?

There are many unanswered questions in the events that followed the murder of Abraham Lincoln, questions which could be answered best only by Edwin M. Stanton, who was in charge during those crucial hours.

Why he refused for hours to identify the killer; why

he finally sent out the wrong picture for that of John Booth; why he perjured himself on the witness stand about the killer's diary; why he refused to let Mr. Lincoln be guarded that fateful night by the man whom the President requested; why he failed to investigate the fact that detailed stories of the assassination were published in two newspapers many hours before the deed; why Lt. Baker was not identified as the killer of Booth, whom he had been ordered to bring back alive!

If we knew the answers to those questions, we might know what prompted Robert Todd Lincoln to burn some of his father's letters. Teddy Roosevelt asked why he was burning letters that might have historical significance. Robert Lincoln replied, "It would serve no purpose to make them public. They deal with a man who played a part in my father's death, a member of father's cabinet."

62

Fantastic Photos

Making photographs by lightning flashes is a stunt so simple that it can be done with box cameras; but when lightning begins making its own photographs—that's a riddle for the experts.

How it is done, nobody knows, but occasionally lightning engraves photographs with remarkable clarity—and with surprising effects on passersby.

On the road between Cleveland and Chattanooga, Tennessee, in 1887, there lived an elderly widow known to the village of Ooltewah as Granny Osborne. Bedfast, she clung to life in the humble cottage where she and her husband had lived for so many years as they scratched out a meagre living from the stony farm.

A few hours before her death, she had managed to lift herself to one elbow in order to watch a violent thunderstorm that was rocking the valley with its fury. Suddenly one great bolt of lightning shattered a pine tree that stood across the road from her house. Granny sank back to her pillow, folded her hands, and passed away.

The surprise came when neighbors who had come to lay her out discovered to their horror that Granny seemed to be peering out the window at them, complete with her frilly night cap and her toothless grin. Examination disclosed that somehow a remarkable likeness of the old lady was embedded in the glass of the window pane where she had watched her last storm; a photographic likeness which newsmen described as comparable in detail to any camera work, except that it was etched by some unknown process on ordinary window glass, where it was visible for years until it finally faded.

The case of Granny Osborne is similar in many respects to one that occurred in Washington, D. C. in 1903, when guests at a dinner party discovered two amazing photographic images embedded in a big plate glass window overlooking the garden; a window that had been covered for years by a paneled mirror. The likenesses were those of an elderly, robust man and a frail and very old lady.

When the former owners of the property were informed of the discovery, they came to investigate, and promptly identified the strange pictures as life-like images of their father and grandmother, both of whom had been dead for many years. They had enjoyed watching electrical storms by standing before this plate glass window which afforded an excellent view; but how their photographs became embedded in thick plate glass was a mystery that even the experts at the Smithsonian could not solve.

The glass was carefully removed and taken to the museum for lengthy examination, but the scientists could only admit that somehow lightning had induced the images into the glass, clear and remarkably lifelike and utterly unexplainable. The glass was catalogued and filed. Somewhere among the Institution's thirty million properties it remains.

At New Albany, Indiana, a Mrs. Sophia Scharf died at

her home at East Fifth and Spring Streets on December 2, 1891. The funeral services were held three days later; and, on the day following the funeral, the dead woman's daughter-in-law went to the house to get some belongings. She was badly frightened when she found the face of the dead woman staring at her from the front window. For about a week the likeness was there, clear and distinct, then, as abruptly as it had appeared, it vanished.

A few weeks later it came back—dimly at first and then more distinctly. All who saw it agreed that it was an excellent likeness of the deceased, but why it was on the clear glass of the big front window no one could explain. Various attempts were made to scrub it off, without success. Finally, a son of Mrs. Scharf, who had belatedly arrived from California for the funeral, merely took his handkerchief and passed it over the picture, and it was gone, never to return.

More permanent, but just as puzzling, was the transformation that occurred in a three-paned window at the home of Jesse Smith, an aged farmer who lived six miles west of Demossville, Kentucky, in the early spring of 1865. The Civil War was dragging to a close, and Smith, like all his neighbors, was waiting for some word from the front. One morning, after a severe storm, Smith and his wife were astounded to see a brilliant rainbow in full color, a band about six inches wide, that arched across the three lower panes of their front window. It was visible only from the outside of the house, but there was no mistaking its presence nor the bright colors that comprised it. The rainbow was *in* the glass, for when the window was raised, the rainbow went with it.

Its appearance created near panic, and hundreds came

to see it and to try to connect it as some sort of omen having to do with the war. In a few days the war ended, but the rainbow remained, still bright and colorful as it was twenty years later when the Cincinnati Enquirer investigated. —Another documented enigma Stranger Than Science.

63

Mysteries On The Moon

The man-made satellites twinkling as they circle the earth day after day and night after night are equipped with instruments which send down information on heat and cold and radio activity in space, but they also send another message which will, in the long run, change the future of the human race.

The existence of these man-made satellites tells us that we are standing on the threshold of space travel, and that the day is near when men for the first time will leave this earth to roam the endless void of the universe. In all probability, we will prepare a manned space station, circling the earth, as a stepping stone from which to launch our journey to the next logical basing point on the moon.

For centuries science has blithely assumed that the moon is a desolate orb bereft of atmosphere, alternately burned by the sunlight and frozen by the absolute zero of darkness; and under such conditions, we are told, the moon could only be a sphere without life of any kind. But many things have happened in recent years to cast doubt on that theory of a lifeless moon.

The evidence is not conclusive, but still strong enough that President Eisenhower's board of scientific advisors cautioned him against firing any nuclear war heads to the moon until, as they expressed it, the existence of some form of life there has been definitely determined.

Life on that stony, forbidding orb without atmosphere, without water? Why did those eminent scientists venture such a cautious warning? Well, let's look at the record. On the night of July 29, 1953, the late John O'Neil, the distinguished science editor of the New York Herald Tribune settled himself at his telescope for an evening's observation of the moon. He slipped an eyepiece with a magnifying power of ninety times into the telescope and squinted at the lunar orb. He could hardly believe his senses! Stretching across the edge of a great barren expanse known as Mare Crisium was the shadow of a bridge-like structure. From pediment to pediment it was at least twelve miles long. Switching eyepieces, he raised the magnification to two hundred and fifty times, and under this higher magnification the gigantic structure appeared sharply in outline. An incredible engineering feat which had apparently been erected in a remarkably short time, for he had not seen it when he examined that same area of the moon only five weeks before.

O'Neil was intelligent enough to know that he would be attacked for reporting such an astounding sight; but he was also courageous enough to make the report. First he told it in detail to the Association of Lunar and Planetary Observers, carefully referring to the object as a great natural bridge. As expected, he was quickly attacked by some astronomers, and at the height of the assault upon his sanity and his veracity, O'Neil was rescued by support from an unassailable source. Dr. H. P. Wilkins, probably the world's outstanding authority on the moon, calmly announced in August of 1953, just one month after O'Neil's discovery, that he, too, had clearly seen the same unmistakable bridge-like structure just where O'Neil had said it was. And the following month, another eminent English lunar authority, Patrick Moore, added his voice in support of O'Neil. He, too, had seen the bridge and had seen it distinctly for more than an hour.

Actually, mysterious configurations on the moon are not unknown—they are merely unexplained. O'Neil's bridge, as we have said, was located in Mare Crisium. And Mare Crisium is no stranger to strange sights.

In 1869 after a series of bright points of light in geometric patterns had been seen, the Royal Astronomical Society assigned to scores of astronomers the task of observing and recording this amazing phenomenon. In a two-year period, they recorded more than a hundred such light patterns, rectangles, straight lines, triangles—many of them around the Mare Crisium. If they were signals to us, their meaning was lost on those who studied them, and in late 1871 the lights ceased to appear.

In 1912, American astronomer F. B. Harris reported watching a gigantic black object, estimated to be fifty miles in diameter, moving across the moon; and so close to the moon that it cast a shadow on the lunar surface. On March 30, 1950, famed British astronomer, Dr. Percy Wilkins, picked up a weird glow near Aristarchus. He describes it as oval-shaped, glowing, and seemingly hovering near the floor of the crater. And three months later, Dr. James Bartlett, Jr., an American astronomer, sighted a similar object at the same spot.

To the growing list of moon phenomena which suggest that sentient beings may be there already, we must add the

257

more than two hundred white circular dome-shaped objects which have been spotted on the moon in recent years. Sometimes these domes vanish from one place, only to appear in another. If these markings on the moon are not artificial, then they constitute a natural phenomenon without parallel.

64

*The Riddle of
The Rainmaker*

In two blazing hot years only two inches of rain had fallen on the parched earth around San Diego. By January of 1916, the city was on the brink of disaster for want of water. It had been three months since the last feeble shower. The reservoirs were virtually dry. Something had to be done, and done quickly.

At the risk of being regarded as idiots, the beleaguered city council voted to employ the services of a professional rainmaker. They had been bombarded with proposals from one Charles Mallory Hatfield, a former sewing machine salesman who claimed he could induce rain, for a fee. He got the job.

With Hatfield, the rains came C.O.D.

He had noticed, he said, that after great battles there were often great storms. He had also noticed that during great battles clouds of cannon smoke rose into the skies; and, to Hatfield, this constituted evidence that the burnt powder had, as he put it, upset the balance of nature in the air. Once upset, clouds formed and rain fell, said Hatfield.

For several years he had experimented on his father's farm in Kansas, setting up huge wooden tubs on towers . . . tubs from which clouds of chemical vapors drifted aloft. Rains came . . . torrential rains sometimes . . . and Hatfield found there were those who would pay him for his services.

For example, the farmers of the San Joaquin valley hired him year after year to provide them with bountiful rains. They paid him ten thousand dollars a year and were happy with the results. The miners of Dawson City, Alaska, paid him $21,000 to torment the skies into providing water for their dry sluiceboxes; and his efforts were followed by four inches of rain.

So, when San Diego finally turned to him in its hour of trial in January of 1916, it was not dealing with an unknown. On the day they hired him, he was dismantling his towers in a valley in northern California where eighteen inches of rain had followed his efforts to "upset the balance of nature."

If he could do half as well for San Diego, the city would be saved. And if he failed, it would be no worse off than before—just thirstier.

San Diego's main source of supply was Lake Morena, a man-made reservoir which had never been more than one-third full in its twenty years' existence. When Hatfield arrived on the scene, the lake level was below the danger point . . . a hot, stinking mudhole and no more. He had made the city two offers: One thousand dollars an inch for each inch of rain that followed his efforts; or for ten thousand dollars, he would fill the lake that had never been filled—fill it with eighteen billion gallons of water— enough to last the city two years if it never rained another drop.

For several days the city council stalled, vainly hoping that nature would provide the water and get them out of their predicament. But when the fourth day dawned as hot and cloudless as its predecessors, they hired Hatfield;

and he put the workmen to setting up his tall wooden towers.

Within twenty-four hours after those towers began sending their evil smelling vapors into the skies, rain began to fall. Crowds stood in the streets to cheer Hatfield. Farmers drove in the rain to the edge of Lake Morena to shake his hand. But the rejoicing didn't last long. On the third consecutive day of rain, the San Diego Exposition was washed out; the Tia Juana race track was flooded.

The city council called Hatfield to see if he couldn't taper off the torrents. On the following day, sixteen dogs drowned in the city pound; ranchers were being rescued in lifeboats; and the weatherman admitted that for the first time in the history of the city he was unable to make a forecast. Telegraph and telephone lines were down . . . railroad bridges were swept away . . . and still the rains came.

Otay and Sweetwater reservoirs filled . . . overflowed . . . and finally burst their earthen dams and thundered down the valley . . . a fifty-foot wall of water that carried fifty persons to their deaths.

Troops were called in for emergency duty . . . Lake Morena filled and overflowed for the first time in its history . . . just as Hatfield had predicted. Then he turned off his towers and went to collect his money. The city, busy digging out of the flood, refused to pay him, and years later his lawsuit was finally dismissed.

Scientists declared that he was a fraud and that his method was worthless and ineffective. But before Hatfield died in 1958, he lived to see scientists making rain by sending chemical vapors into the air, just as he had done forty years before.

65

Specimens From
The Sky

If the sky looks empty, it is being deceptive, for the record of material that falls from the sky is so varied it is almost unbelievable. But the evidence is there, even though the answers aren't.

The date was December 22, 1955. William Shannon and George Brinsmaid, professional illustrators, were driving to work at the RCA Service Company in Alexandria, Virginia, in Brinsmaid's car. They were on the smooth, winding Mt. Vernon Highway when, as they both reported—"all of a sudden there was a terrific bang and a big hole in the windshield." What's more, there was a big frozen fish, ten inches long, on the floor of the car. It had come straight down, like a bomb, with terrific force—enough velocity to knock a hole a foot square in the shatter-proof glass and to crack the windshield all the way across.

There were no cars around, no airplanes, and no explanation. Just the frozen fish, the broken windshield, and two badly rattled men who turned around and drove right back home.

Having beeen taught that the sky does not contain

fish, frozen or otherwise, we are understandably reluctant to accept the evidence at face value. As late as 1805, astronomers ridiculed the idea that stones and chunks of iron actually fell from the sky upon occasion. There were no stones in the skies, therefore they could not fall from the skies. It was that simple, until Biot, the famed physicist and academician, investigated a fall of stones in 1805 and declared that they had, indeed, fallen from the skies, just as the ignorant peasants had been saying for years.

Brinsmaid and Shannon were bombarded with that frozen fish in December of 1955, another oddity that can't happen, but it did. So it was with huge chunks of ice that battered automobiles on July 4, 1953, in Long Beach, California. American Avenue there is automobile row and that seemed to be the target. Three parked cars were badly damaged by chunks of crystal clear ice that came whistling down from a clear sky.

At 1480 American Avenue, the used car lot of L. A. Smith caught a blockbuster—a heavy chunk that struck a car with such force that the hood and fender were knocked off and the motor exposed. An employee, H. A. Boyd, told the Los Angeles Examiner: "I had just finished polishing that car and I was about fifty feet away when I heard a sizzing sound. I looked up and saw the air full of big shiny stuff plunging down. A big piece of ice that looked about the size of a man smashed down on that car and ice flew all over the lot."

Diagonally across the street from the scene of that ice fall, a former P-38 pilot, Charles Roscoe, was sitting in his office when he heard the crash. He told authorities later: "It sounded like a gun blast so I ran out to see what it was. Just as I reached the door of my office at 1416 American Avenue, something hit the roof of the office with a wham like a big rock. I looked up and I could see the sun shining on big pieces coming from 2000 feet up. They rolled and turned in the air like a kind of waterfall. I looked for a plane, but there wasn't any."

The meteorologists promptly dismissed the whole thing as chunks of ice from a plane; but their explanation is dismissed as worthless by aviation authorities who point out that it is impossible for ice in such massive chunks to form on any plane . . . nor could any plane have dropped so much ice in the same place for two minutes.

But the ice was there, even if the planes weren't.

In 1921, white shining material that looked like pieces of polished chinaware came tinkling down at Portland, Oregon, accompanied by sizeable chunks of ice, all of it falling into an area about one hundred feet square.

Hundreds of pounds of shredded flesh fell on the property of an amazed and annoyed rancher named Hudson, in Los Nietos Township, California, on August 9, 1869. The flesh was in very thin flakes and strips, from the size of a dollar to the size of a man's hand. It was freshly cut when it fell but soon became putrid. Investigators noted that it had fine black bristles on one edge, but they could not offer any explanation as to where it came from or how it drifted down from the sky on Mr. Hudson's ranch.

On March 3, 1876, in Bath County, Kentucky, there was a fall of what the investigators from a college in Lexington described as "half a wagon load of pieces of fresh meat, sliced into thin strips, some of it quite bloody, all of it strung out across two hillside fields on the same farm in a band about fifty feet wide and about three hundred feet long." Witnesses had seen it drifting down from the sky—the empty sky that holds so many strange things such as rocks and chunks of iron and huge cakes of ice—and sometimes fresh meat.

We have hardly scratched the surface of the astounding list of things that have fallen from the skies, many of them in recent years. Unable to explain them, science does the next best thing . . . it ignores them.

66

The Curse of
The Scharnhorst

German sailors were patriotic, but not idiotic. They claimed that the Scharnhorst was jinxed, and they avoided her like the plague. She was forty thousand tons of fighting fury, and she was also a hoodooed battle cruiser.

Hitler's scientists put everything they had into this sleek new craft. They gave her speed to outrun the heavier British dreadnaughts. They armed her with long-range rifles that could seek out the enemy over the horizon and powerful electronic gear to find her targets before *they* found *her*.

The first indication that she was a troublemaker came when the Scharnhorst was only two-thirds completed. With little more than a hoarse moan of crumbling timbers, she rolled over on her side, crushing to death sixty-one workmen and injuring a hundred and ten others.

Raising her took three months. Crews of workmen had to be drafted; for it was whispered that this sleek steel monster was jinxed, as indeed she may have been.

At long last came the day for the launching. All the Nazi bigwigs were there: Hitler, Himmler, Goering, Scheirich, Hess, and Doenitz. They were going to make this launching a major occasion with which to impress their jittery neighbors by their skill at contriving new and deadlier weapons. All the top Nazis were there—but one of the principals was missing—the Scharnhorst!

During the night, the Scharnhorst had launched herself, grinding up a pair of barges as she lurched toward the channel. To conceal their embarrassment, the Nazis claimed that the launching had been held the night before in order to conceal a secret launching system.

Hoodoo and all, Hitler's pride was finally afloat.

When the Germans seized Danzig, they sent out news-films all over the world, showing the mighty Scharnhorst pumping hundreds of tons of death and destruction into the helpless port. But they failed to mention that during the attack on Danzig, the Scharnhorst had murdered nine of her own men when one of her big guns exploded. When the air system quit working, she suffocated twelve gunners in another turret.

Again the Scharnhorst lived up to her evil tradition during the siege of Oslo. While the Nazi battleships poured their shells into the hapless port, the Scharnhorst took far more than her share of the hits. Aflame in a dozen places, she had to be pulled to safety by the Gneisenau.

She made poor time limping home, for she had to hide from the British bombers by day and creep along the coast by night. Thus it was that one black night she finally entered the Elbe on the last leg of her journey to safety.

For some reason her radar failed to reveal the presence of the world's largest ocean liner squarely in her path in the darkness. The watch sounded the alarm, but too late, for seconds later he died in the collision; and the mighty Bremen settled into the mud to spend the rest of the war as a sitting duck for the Allied bombers.

By the time repairs had been made and the Scharnhorst was again ready for service, Hitler's star was fading. The gigantic Bismarck had gone down under air and sea attack; the Tirpitz was lying in a Norwegian fjord, gutted by torpedoes. Hitler had no choice but to send the Scharnhorst into action, jinx and all.

Once more she slipped down the Elbe at night, past the bomb-blasted hulk of the Bremen and northward along the coast of Norway on her way to a hit-and-run attack on an allied convoy in the Arctic sea. It looked like a cinch, and for another ship it might have been.

The same blackness that hid the Scharnhorst from British planes also hid the crippled British patrol boat from the Scharnhorst. The battle cruiser thundered past, a few hundred yards from the little craft that was paralyzed by disabled engines, and never saw it. But the warning was flashed. Within minutes, a British fleet had wheeled about; driving full speed toward its target.

The Scharnhorst was too fast for her lumbering adversaries, and after a few shots she fled from them in the inky blackness. The British commander took a chance and fired a broadside at 16,000 yards, and the ill-fated Scharnhorst swung directly into the path of the tons of high explosive that staggered her. More hits followed quickly and the stricken vessel plunged to the bottom.

Most of the crew died in the icy water, but two of them managed to reach shore in a flimsy rubber raft. There they were found months later, dead from the explosion of their tiny emergency oil heater. They had eluded the British and the raging sea—but they couldn't escape the jinx of the Scharnhorst.

67

Murder By Hypnotism

Can one human being dominate the mind of another and drive the subject to commit a crime by will power alone—through hypnosis? Science says NO, but the court called it "murder by hypnotism."

Here is the story —

In his thirty-three years, Palle Hardrupp had never been in trouble. The gun in his coat pocket felt cold and unwieldy. He walked past the bank four times, like a man in a stupor, fondling the gun with one hand, holding his coat collar up around his throat with the other hand; for March 29, 1951, was a raw day in Copenhagen.

It was a small bank that Palle had chosen for his crime, or perhaps it would be more nearly correct to say that it was a small bank that had been chosen for him. Time after time the hypnotist had told Palle to get a gun and go to that bank. Get a gun and go to that bank! Now, benumbed and fumbling, Palle was stopped in front of the bank—a gun in his pocket.

His mind was fighting a losing battle against the will of another as Palle stumbled into the bank and approached the first window. Cashier Kaj Moller looked up and smiled

—but the smile froze on his lips when he saw the strange mad light in Hardrupp's eyes. Palle doesn't know whether he asked for money—and Kaj Moller will never tell—for the gun that was staring him in the face roared twice and Moller fell dead.

The other bank employees fell behind their counters—the customers ran out the front door—only Hans Wisbom, a bank manager, dared face the gunman. He paid for his temerity with his life—sprawled on the floor with a bullet in his brain. Palle Hardrupp stared stupidly at his latest victim before he stuck the gun back in his pocket and stumbled out of the bank, muttering to himself.

When he came to trial for the double murder, Palle had a strange story to tell. He related to the jury how he had submitted to hypnosis at the hands of Bjorn Nielsen, and how Nielsen had told him three times a week for three months that he must rob this bank, even though he did not want to rob it or any other bank, and that he must shoot the cashier if he failed to give him the money; although he did not want to shoot anybody, for any reason.

Under this cumulative compulsion, Palle told the jury he had found himself little more than a zombie, a living creature who had lost control of his will, forced to do a crime he could not avoid.

Although the jury accepted Nielsen's claim that he had not been near the scene of the crime when it was committed, the jury also believed Palle Hardrupp's story that he had been a mere robot directed by Nielsen's will power, applied through hypnotism. Nielsen was indicted for planning the robbery and for instigating the murders.

Such a charge was unprecedented; for, in order to prove its case, the government of Denmark had to prove that

Nielsen had deliberately chosen to force Hardrupp to commit a crime of violence against his will, and had repeatedly hypnotized Hardrupp in order to condition his mind to accept the order to commit the crime. It was going to be difficult; for it is generally held that hypnosis cannot be used to compel or induce a person to perform an act which he would not willfully perform when not hypnotized.

Two fine citizens had died at the hands of the hypnotist's subject! Could the state prove that Nielsen had caused their deaths by his skill as a hypnotist?

The trial was a sensation in many aspects. As expected, Palle Hardrupp was found guilty of the murders and the attempted bank theft. He was sentenced to a home for psychopaths, from which he would be eligible for release in two years, provided he showed a recovery from the condition existing at the time of the crime.

But Nielsen was an entirely different case. It required expert witnesses with convincing testimony, if he were to be convicted. Dr. Paul Reiter, former governor of the Denmark insane asylum and later head of the psychiatric department of the Copenhagen City Hospital, was the chief witness for the state. He testified that in committing the crime Hardrupp had acted contrary to his normal reasoning and desires; had acted, in fact, in an insane, semi-conscious condition while deprived of his own free will by repeated hypnotic suggestive influence; driven to criminal impulse by compulsion from without.

Furthermore, said Dr. Reiter, any person can be capable of any act, and a hypnotist can induce most persons to commit crime by repeatedly presenting the crime as having a worthy purpose. In the case of Hardrupp, the state showed that Nielsen had cunningly convinced his dupe

271

that the money from the bank robbery would be used to fight communism.

Other eminent psychiatrists supported Dr. Reiter. Under psychiatric examination, Nielsen admitted he bore the moral responsibility for the crime; that he had conceived the plot to test his hypnotic powers.

Bjorn Nielsen got a sentence of life imprisonment for the unprecedented crime of committing murder by hypnotism.

68

Post Mortem
Explorer

For centuries men sought a passage around the Arctic Ocean between the Atlantic and the Pacific, the famed Northwest Passage. But the man who finally found it—never knew it! . . .

Many a career was wrecked and many a fortune lost, in the search for a deepwater passage between the North American continent and the Arctic Ocean—"the Northwest Passage"—as it was called, which would be a short cut between Europe and the riches of the Orient. It was worth the gamble, of course, since it promised undying fame for the explorer who discovered the route, and great wealth for the nation that backed him.

But strangely enough, history does not mention the first man who made the trip from ocean to ocean north of land, and perhaps not so strangely, he made no claim to the honor. It's a most unusual story; it would be quite incredible if it were not so well documented.

On the morning of August 12, 1775, the American whaling ship Herald was cruising off the west coast of Greenland, well above the Arctic Circle. Whaling was poor and a double lookout had been posted to prevent any possible oversight of such quarry as might be in the area. Hour after hour the Herald slipped along through an empty sea. But not quite empty; for from among the towering icebergs that dotted the frigid waters the lookouts spied a three-masted schooner, apparently drifting aimlessly. What few sails were visible were tattered rags; the coating of ice on the spars glistened pinkly in the morning sun.

When she first appeared, the strange ship was three or four miles away, drifting before a light breeze. Captain Warren ordered the Herald hove to until the eerie visitor should come close enough to hail. But the hail produced no reply. There were no signs of life on the other vessel. Captain Warren took eight men and a longboat and rowed over to the stranger. Time and the elements had almost erased her name but Warren was still able to make it out, the Octavius. He had never heard of her.

Pulling alongside, Warren hailed her again, and again he was greeted with a deep and abiding silence. It was spooky. When none of the men would agree to board the vessel with him, Warren selected four men and ordered them to come along. Leading the way himself, the five of them scrambled up the rotten ropes that dangled overside, rigging that had fallen long before. Once aboard the Octavius they had to proceed with caution for the decks were rotten and covered with slimy green moss. The ship's wheel was unattended. Below decks the boarding party recoiled in horror. In the crew's quarters they found the bodies of twenty-eight men, all heavily bundled in their bunks . . . and all perfectly preserved by the Arctic cold.

Fumbling their way aft to the Captain's cabin they found the body of the vessel's master slumped in his chair at his work table, head bent forward, his pen lying beside his hand as though he had gone to sleep at his work. His face and hands were covered with a thin greenish mold but otherwise the body was well preserved. Behind the Captain in his cabin, a woman had frozen to death in the bed, her body heavily wrapped in blankets.

In the corner of the room a sailor sat cross-legged, leaning back slightly into the corner, flint and steel still clutched in his hands . . . the little pile of shavings before him mute evidence of the task he had attempted and failed. Beside him, face buried in the folds of the sailor's jacket was a small boy, huddling for the warmth that wasn't there. Captain Warren and his men removed their hats, offered a prayer for the dead and crept up the rickety companionway, taking the log book with them.

Back aboard his own vessel Captain Warren watched the derelict drift on out of sight among the icebergs. Turning to the log book of the Octavius, he found the final entry dated November 11, 1762. It told how the ship had been frozen in for seventeen days . . . the fire had gone out . . . the captain had tried to rekindle it and failed . . . so he had given the flint and steel to the first mate. The crew, said the log book, was anxiously awaiting the kindling of the fire, for the cold was sheer agony. The location of the ship . . . Longitude 160 W, Latitude 75 N. Captain Warren read it again to make sure he was seeing it correctly and checked it with his own officers. They agreed with him. The Octavius, on its day of doom, had been frozen in the Arctic Ocean at a point north of Point Barrow, Alaska—thousands of miles from where Captain Warren had found it!

Somehow, miraculously, the ship had survived the onslaught of the elements and had crept, year by year, eastward thru the vast ice field until it eventually entered the North Atlantic, where Captain Warren found it. The Octavius had been the first ship to negotiate the historic Northwest Passage, with a captain and a crew that had been dead for 13 years!

69

The Killer Comets

In late 1958, the news services quoted several top government meteorologists as saying that their research has led them to believe that the world's weather was subject to influence by cosmic dust, the clouds of microscopic particles through which the earth passes from time to time in its mad rush through space.

We know that rain and snow both require triggering action; in other words, tiny particles around which the droplets of moisture can first form before they evolve into rain or snow. We also know that billions of tiny particles enter our atmosphere on any average day, while on those occasions when the earth spins through a cloud or even a thin layer of cosmic dust, the conditions are then right for rainfall of unpredictable quantity, provided the moisture is in the air when the dust arrives.

Astronomers have learned that the spectacular tails of comets are extremely tenuous bodies, composed of such minute particles that the pressure of light can bend them. From time to time the earth passes through such masses of space material—through comet tails—and sometimes with unpleasant results, which may or may not be mere coincidence.

Even among the ancients, the possible relationship between comets and plagues had been noted. The Bible, in the first chapter of Chronicles, tells how King David was hiding on the threshing floor at Ornam when his terrified followers beheld a great comet, dragging behind it a flaming tail that filled the sky, and soon afterward a great pestilence broke out, taking the lives of 70,000 persons.

In 1665, another spectacular comet made its appearance, sweeping in regal splendor through the heavens and leaving a tail through which the earth also passed. Again, perhaps by sheer coincidence, a pestilence ravished the world . . . the infamous Black Plague which killed millions and which decimated the populations of cities and continents.

Modern science has identified many diseases as being air-borne, the work of tiny creatures, some of which are so small that they can be detected only by the fantastic magnification of an electron microscope. It is also known that many of the germs can survive freezing without apparent harm to themselves.

If these things are present in the dust of space, including the dust of comet trails, it is by no means illogical to suspect that they not only trigger weather, but epidemics, as the ancients believed. And since some races are more resistant to certain diseases than other races, the epidemics would not ravage all alike. An example of this racial immunity is evidenced by the bubonic plague which killed hundreds of thousands of people in India in 1896 and '97, while Europeans there moved freely through the plague areas with almost no difficulty.

But from time to time, diseases appear with dramatic suddenness and sweep around the world, sparing neither race nor color. Such a killer was the Black Death of 1347 which followed soon after the comet and seemed to have struck the whole earth at the same time, killing about half of all th. inhabitants of the earth in three terrible years.

Daniel Webster survived an influenza epidemic that took a heavy toll of life, here and abroad, and it was he who called attention to the appearance of the disease following the near approach of a comet. He may have been mis-interpreting the facts—and then again, he may not.

Spectroscopic analysis of comet tails discloses that they contain great quantities of gases, including some that are deadly to human beings. From time to time we pass through the tails of comets without knowing it, and admittedly at such times our atmosphere absorbs some of the gases as well as some of the dust.

Research has been conducted relative to the long-range effects of small amounts of lethal gases on the tissues of living creatures. Does it condition them to such an extent that they fall prey to common diseases which they would otherwise be able to resist? Does the slow seepage of cosmic dust and cosmic gases through our atmosphere play a part in preparing the human race for epidemics?

The history of the human race is replete with epidemics and with comets. Whether they are related, no man can say, but man has long feared both of them—perhaps with good reason!

70

A Living Miracle

Each year on Good Friday the stigmatists' wounds appear and bleed as did the wounds of Christ on the cross—a scientific impossibility that happens with disturbing regularity—a phenomenon stranger than science.

Down thru the centuries literally hundreds of persons known as stigmatists have displayed the phenomenon that involves such wounds. That it does happen, and is still happening, is a matter of lengthy public record, but no one knows how or why.

In almost every case the stigmatist has been a very devout person, extremely sensitive and generally quite emotional. These factors have led many investigators to contend that the stigmata are the results of the remarkable control of mind over body, that the mind of the stigmatist wills the body to break open and bleed as it does.

It's an interesting theory but nothing more; for equally eminent scholars who have investigated declare that the mind over body supposition is inadequate and in some instances, impossible.

There the argument stands. Now let's examine the evidence.

The two most famous living stigmatists are Theresa Neumann, who lives quietly in Konnersreuth, Germany, and Padre Pio, of the monastery of San Giovanni Rotondo, in southeast Italy. Temperamentally quite dissimilar, these two remarkable people share the same physical oddity, that of bleeding wounds corresponding to those of the crucifixion. For Miss Neumann this has been a condition with which she has coped since 1926 when they first appeared on her body. Like the wounds on Padre Pio, they never heal, neither do they ever become infected.

Tens of thousands of American GI's visited Padre Pio during World War II. They found him to be a rather stout little man with a pleasant, almost happy-go-lucky outlook on life. Then, as for many years past, his wounds bled continually. Padre Pio has the unusual distinction of having all five of the crucifixion marks, one in each hand and each foot, plus a gash in his side, about three inches long, which saturates from three to five handkerchiefs per day. He is the first regularly ordained Catholic priest on record to bear all five of the stigmata.

Padre Pio was born Francis Forgione in the Italian province of Benevento in 1887. He was one of a large peasant family. As a boy he showed evidence of extreme piety and in his early teens he joined the Franciscan order of Friars to study for the priesthood.

There was nothing physically unusual about him until the morning of September 20, 1918. On that morning, as usual, he began the day by praying. Suddenly he felt faint and lost consciousness. When he next opened his eyes he discovered that his hands and feet appeared to be pierced and bleeding, a fact which he tried to conceal, although he was quite mystified by it. A few minutes later he discovered that a wound in his side was also bleeding quite freely.

Brother monks summoned doctors, who treated the wounds but were unable to stop the flow of blood. Examination showed that Padre Pio had holes entirely through both hands and both feet and that the gash in his side was several inches deep. All the wounds were permanent and, from that day to this, they have continued to flow in spite of persistent efforts to cauterize or to heal them.

To the Catholic authorities the news of the stigmatization of roly-poly Padre Pio was but a new chapter in an old, old story. Over the centuries more than 300 stigmatists has been recorded, most of them nuns or friars. In accordance with a long established policy in such cases the Church ordered Padre Pio not to appear in public for two years.

During this period he was the subject of intensive study by both medical and ecclesiastical authorities and when they had finished their investigations he was again permitted to make public appearances. The summary of the investigations held that the wounds were permanent and unquestionably present, and that his exceptionally humble and Christian way of life entitled him to special consideration.

As a safeguard against sensationalism he is under orders not to reveal his stigmata unless special permission is granted. Generally Padre Pio wears thin brown gloves over the wounds on his hands, gloves which he removes when he says mass. Like Theresa Neumann, the flow of blood from his wounds is heaviest on Good Fridays, as countless witnesses have testified.

Science is at a loss for an acceptable explanation to the

strange wounds of the stigmatists. Thorough investigation has ruled out the possibility of fraud.

As the fame of Padre Pio spread around the world, with it spread news of the thousands who came to ask him to pray for them in their illnesses, and today a modern hospital stands next door to his monastery—a hospital named for the late Mayor LaGuardia of New York City, who helped to provide funds for it.

Padre Pio, who was seventy-two in 1959, visits the sick each day; a kindly, devout man whose strange wounds have caused millions to regard him as a living miracle that science can not yet explain.

71

A Voice From
The Dead?

Is it possible for the dead to express themselves through the physical bodies of persons in hypnotic trance? Science, for the most part, promptly answers "No!", which is to be expected, but science admittedly has no answer for such cases as that of Patricia Kord.

Fortunately the new tape recorder was working perfectly as Miss Kord, a twenty-eight-year-old university secretary, lay in deep trance on that somber November afternoon in 1957 in her parents' home in Indianapolis. The hypnotist was her uncle, Richard Cook, and he had often given her hypnotic treatment for her frequent headaches.

This time was destined to be different.

The girl suddenly sank into an unusually deep trance. Her slow breathing became laborious, her pulse rate dropped alarmingly. From her lips came a voice which neither Cook nor her parents had ever heard before—a voice which claimed to be that of a young Confederate soldier named Gene Donaldson.

Slowly the voice told how he had been working on his parents' farm near Shreveport, Louisiana, one hot summer afternoon when a big wagon came along, filled with young men on their way to join the rebels. Gene told how he went with them, down the Red River on a flatboat, up the Yazoo as far as they dared go and then at last to his first engagement, the battle of Shiloh, where his buddy was killed and where he was blinded in one eye by a Yankee bullet.

Cook asked the voice if he had any medical care.

"I don't 'member no doctors. Not at Shiloh, sir. Never saw no doctors till the battle of Nashville, a long time later."

"Was the battle of Nashville worse than Shiloh?"

"Oh, yes, sir! There was more men—and there was more dead ones—they was everywhere at Nashville."

Little by little, Cook's questioning brought forth a detailed story of the alleged childhood of this voice which called itself Gene Donaldson: How he had spent his childhood and young manhood on that farm near Shreveport, the people he knew, his neighbors (and some unflattering comments about some of them) the stores at which his family traded, the little bank run by Mr. Emmonds, the church and various other odds and ends which might possibly be verified even at this late date.

Richard Cook, the amateur hypnotist, carefully recorded these proceedings on tape. The voice had mentioned briefly that Gene Donaldson, by that time a corporal in the Confederate Army, had been killed in the battle of Nashville. Efforts to draw out the details of his death were met with evasion, until finally, in a subsequent experiment, Cook induced the voice to talk about the matter.

The voice told how Gene Donaldson, the naive country boy had evolved into a corporal in charge of a Confederate cannon on the heights near Nashville, then—

"We ran outta cannon balls. We never had nothin' to shoot. They was a Yankee gun on the next ridge—"

"A cannon, do you mean? A Yankee cannon?"

"Yes, sir. We can't fight without no gun. I was gonna see—if I could run around that ridge and git that gun— 'cause we didn't have nothin' to fire back—they was killin' our men and couldn't fire back . . . I was runnin' down that ridge . . . and I couldn't see outta my eye . . . I ain't had no seein' in that one eye since Shiloh. I'm runnin' along that ridge best as I could . . . when somebody shot me in the side—"

"When you were shot were you able to continue?"

"I fell down . . ." (sigh and silence)

"Go ahead, please. Did you get any help?"

"They w'ant no help to git! They was an awful lot of dead ones—no help for none of us."

"Were you able to help yourself?"

"Just laid there . . . just laid there!" The voice trailed off at this point.

"Go ahead, please! You were just lying there on the ridge where you had been shot. Tell us what happened next."

"It got dark and awful cold. Some stars come out—it was awful cold."

"Did you survive that wound?"

Whisper: "No."

"Did you live to the next morning?"

Whisper (very faint): "No, sir."

"You died, then, during the night? Is that right?"

"Yes."

The voice told haltingly of the aftermath of Gene Donaldson's death; how the bodies, including his, had lain unattended for "long, long days" before burial details finally came to dump them into a common grave.

"Did it seem important to you—what they did with your body? Did you care?"

"No, sir. You don't care where they put you!"

"After you died, did you see anyone you knew? Any of your friends or fellow soldiers or any members of your family?"

"I went back to my Ma. She was in the kitchen . . . but she couldn't hear me, seems like."

Neither the hypnotist, Richard Cook, nor the subject, Patricia Kord, had any explanation to offer for this eerie voice from the void. Neither had ever been to Shreveport and Miss Kord, in fact, had never been south of the Ohio River. Nor had either of them ever heard of the alleged rebel soldier Gene Donaldson. The transcription of the strange voice contained considerable detail, or alleged detail. Much would depend on whether the verifiable details checked with the recordings.

Some months after the event Cook permitted newsmen to hear the tape recordings. Their reports were carried on the front pages of newspapers all over the country, including Nashville, where interested but skeptical newspapers decided to do a bit of investigating.

The probe conducted by the Nashville papers included a search of the Confederate Army records in the national archives in Washington, where they found that a Private Gene Donaldson from Shreveport had indeed enlisted in the Louisiana Volunteers, one of the units that fought both at Shiloh and later at Nashville. Further study of the recordings by historians led them to the belief that the fight in which "Gene Donaldson" claims to have been killed was probably that known as Shy's Hill, one of the minor engagements of the sprawling Nashville battle.

The Shreveport Times reported that records had been found showing that a Donaldson family had indeed owned land near that city as far back as 1811. Other records showed that families named Duncan and N'chols had lived on farms near that of the Donaldsons, just as the voice in the trance had related. There had been a Watters Street in Shreveport, long since forgotten but included in the statements of the alleged rebel soldier, as well as a small bank owned by a Mr. Emmonds, a bank which went out of business during the Civil War.

The strange story told by this voice which purported to be that of a Confederate Corporal who had been dead almost a century is by no means unique except that in this case so much evidence has been uncovered substantiating details mentioned in the narrative.

Voices from subjects in hynotic trance, telling stories which seem to transcend time and distance and even death itself, are not new but they present an unsolved riddle which is indeed Stranger than Science.

72

Spies In The Skies

All over the world, nations are confronted with evidence which indicates that intelligent beings from outer space may already be looking us over.

Alexander the Great was not the first to see them nor was he the first to find them troublesome. He tells of two strange craft that dived repeatedly at his army until the war elephants, the men, and the horses all panicked and refused to cross the river where the incident occurred. What did the things look like? His historian describes them as great shining silvery shields, spitting fire around the rims . . . things that came from the skies and returned to the skies.

At Bonham, Texas, in 1873, workers in a cotton field were terrorized by a shiny, silver object that came streaking down from the sky at them. It swung around, like a great silver serpent, said one witness, and dived at them again and again. A team of horses ran away and the driver was thrown under the wheels of the wagon and killed.

And on the same day, an hour or so after the Bonham incident, the same or a similar thing swooped down from the skies at some Army troops on the cavalry parade ground at Fort Riley, Kansas, and terrorized the horses to such an extent that the cavalry drill ended in tumult.

In broad daylight on April 9, 1897, hundreds of thousands of people throughout the midwest witnessed one of the strangest unexplained celestial spectacles on record. It was the start of a show that lasted for seven thrilling days and nights. Whatever the thing was, it was moving at great height. Through telescopes it appeared to be a cigar-shaped object with broad stubby wings. At night it flashed red, green, and white lights. It was seen both day and night from points as far south as St. Louis and as far west as Denver. Astronomers watched it for several days before it vanished, as suddenly as it had appeared, on April 16.

But it was not gone completely.

In the early morning hours of the 19th of April, 1897, the little town of Sistersville, West Virginia, was aroused from slumber by the frantic blowing of the whistle at the sawmill. The sleepy citizens tumbled from their beds and hurried into the streets, to be greeted with a sight that remains a mystery to this day.

Overhead, slowly circling in the sky, was some kind of great cigar-shaped construction. All agreed that it made a humming sound. Its brilliant searchlights swept around over the countryside, long, dazzling fingers of white light that made the community as bright as midday.

Those who watched it agreed that it was a mammoth construction, tubular in shape, about two hundred feet long, with red and green lights along the sides. After ten minutes of this meandering, the thing switched off the searchlights, whooshed eastward and vanished, leaving behind a badly frightened community where church attendance reached record proportions in the ensuing weeks.

There was nothing known to man that could match its performance; for that was six years before the Wright brothers dared the winds of Kitty Hawk with their feeble flying machines.

Nor was there ever any explanation of the thing that visited Chattanooga one January morning in 1910. This was a cigar-shaped object about a hundred feet long, silvery white, glistening. Along its sides there were no wings, nor was there any visible means of propulsion, although many among the thousands who saw it, reported that they heard a distinct chugging sound.

Whatever it was, it came over the city of Chattanooga at an altitude of about five hundred feet, chugging audibly, moving at an estimated twenty miles per hour. Thousands rushed out to see it. After thrilling the citizens of Chattanooga for a little more than an hour it scudded away, to reappear fifteen minutes later over Huntsville, Alabama, about seventy-five miles away. The following day it again came down out of the overcast and slowly chugged around over the city of Chattanooga. Then, as thousands watched, it rose into the mists over famed Missionary Ridge and vanished forever.

It had joined hundreds of its fellow sky voyagers in their strange procedure of appearing briefly and unmistakably before it vanished in the blue.

Of more recent vintage was the astounding visit of unidentified flying objects which swarmed in the skies over Washington, D.C., on the night of August 13, 1952. Government censorship kept the story from the public until almost two years after the incident itself; then an official government publication admitted the truth, that sixty-eight unidentified flying objects had hovered and zoomed and flipped around over the nation's capitol during that un-forgettable night. Under pressure from scientists who sus-pected the things were space craft, the White House had ordered that no hostile action was to be taken against them.

They came, and they went as they had come—swiftly, silently, and in peace. But where they came from . . . and where they went . . . is a mystery that is Stranger Than Science.

73

Strangers In
The Skies

What are these things the Air Force calls Unidentified Flying Objects, better known as flying saucers? Where do they come from? What do they want? A farmer's wife photographed one as it hovered over her barnyard. Another chased a big passenger airliner. Were they the same object?

On the evening of May 11, 1950, Mr. and Mrs. Paul Trent drove into the yard beside their small farm home near McMinnville, Oregon. It was about 7:30 and, although the sun had set, there was ample afterglow in the sky.

Mr. Trent had some pet rabbits in cages behind the garage and, from time to time, in his absence, dogs had broken into the cages and killed some of the bunnies. Had they done it again? Mr. Trent would have a look.

Suddenly he stopped in his tracks. Over the field behind his garage, a strange object was suspended in mid air. It appeared to be circular in shape, flat on the bottom, with a low flat-topped dome on it. He heard no sound . . . just that thing hovering there over the field and rocking slowly from side to side like a rowboat riding at anchor in quiet water . . . except that this thing was up in the air, at least a hundred feet above the field. As Mrs. Trent came up beside him, he noticed that she still had their little folding camera in her hand; for they had been taking pictures of some children that afternoon. Did she have any film left in the camera? She did . . . and Mrs. Trent promptly snapped a picture of the object that hovered over the field. As she carefully turned the film to the next exposure the object began to move, silently, banking around toward them. She got another picture as it swung past . . . and then . . . in seconds . . . it was gone.

Mrs. Trent did not know it; but she had made two of the finest saucer pictures ever recorded by any civilian— pictures that were to make headlines coast to coast in the weeks ahead.

In fact, neither of the Trents realized what they had seen or photographed. They sent the films to a drugstore to be developed and printed, sorted out the pictures of the children, and thought no more about it.

The McMinnville pictures were made on the evening of May 11, 1950.

Nineteen days later, on the night of Memorial Day, Captain Willis Sperry was at the controls of a big American Airlines DC-6 which roared out of the National Airport in Washington, D.C., en route to Tulsa. The take-off was routine . . . the big four-engined plane was climbing at about 170 miles an hour over Mount Vernon, Virginia, a few minutes after leaving the airport.

Suddenly the co-pilot grabbed Captain Sperry's wrist and pointed dead ahead. There, directly in the path of their plane, a big, dark object lay motionless in mid air. Sperry shoved the wheel forward and nosed the plane down a little, to get better control. The mystery object glistened in the moonlight as it accelerated swiftly and sped a few hundred yards to the left. Was it a night fighter plan. without lights—a violation of all flying regulations?

Captain Sperry flashed a report back to the control tower in Washington. The radar there had picked up the thing on its scope, but it was not a plane. The object moved farther to the left and swung around behind the wing of the airliner. As it did so, both Captain Sperry and the co-pilot got a good look at it in silhouette, clearly outlined against a moonlit cloudbank. It looked, both fliers agreed, "like the conning tower of a small submarine!"

They had little time to ponder this unusual configuration. A few seconds later the co-pilot took the wheel and banked the big plane to the right, for the object had circled the plane and was now on the co-pilot's side. Washington radar was still watching it. "No other planes in the area," it reported. What was the object circling the airliner? Captain Sperry radioed back that it was not a plane. It was like nothing he had ever seen before. Reluctantly he added, "It looks to us like the conning tower of a little submarine!"

Seconds later the object shot across in front of the plane, streaked out toward the Atlantic and vanished in the night.

Captain Sperry took the anticipated ridicule from his fellow pilots when the report of his flying submarine made the newswires. Scoffers merely remarked that the flying saucers were becoming more sensational all the time.

Three weeks later farmer Paul Trent happened to mention to a newspaper editor the pictures Mrs. Trent had taken of that object over their farm. The negatives were found under a sofa where the children had thrown them. New prints were made, and the pictures were published in Life magazine and in newspapers all over the world. And much to Captain Sperry's satisfaction, millions of people noted that the object that hovered over Paul Trent's farm looked, as Captain Sperry had said of the one over Virginia, "like the conning tower of a tiny submarine"—another chapter in the unanswered riddle of the flying saucers.

POSTSCRIPT

The marvels that science cannot explain are not limited to yesterday alone.

They happen every day in all parts of the world.

For example, after I completed the manuscript for this book, the story which follows came to my attention.

I offer it to you as a bonus and as evidence that our new scientific discoveries sometimes only serve to emphasize how truly mysterious are the events that are Stranger Than Science!

Frank Edwards

P.S.

A Guest From The Universe?

The stage was being set for a world-shaking drama that was rushing to its fiery climax near the cold and sluggish Yenesei River of Siberia.

The date: June 30, 1908.

Out in space, miles from the earth, a gigantic object was rushing to destruction, headed for a thinly populated area near the Yenesei. Its speed was probably in excess of thirty thousand miles an hour. It was only seconds from destruction, trailing long streams of fire behind it as it entered the atmosphere.

On the river a fisherman tugged at the ropes leading to his nets. He paused in his work long enough to return the wave of a friend who sat on the shore, sheltered fortunately by a steep overhang. His friend on the bank was the last thing the fisherman would ever see.

He had less than five seconds to live.

A few miles from the river a herdsman, driving several hundred reindeer across the grassy flats, paused to fill his leather water bag at a shallow well. The bag fell into the water and he climbed down to retrieve it.

It was the luckiest move of his life.

Across the river, at the edge of a small grove of trees, a woodchopper and his two grown sons took time out from their labors to smoke their pipes, their axes leaning against the log on which they were sitting.

The stage was set.

The gigantic thing that was plunging to earth exploded with a fury that was recorded around the globe. Of those in the immediate area, only the herdsman in the well and the man sheltered by the river bank survived. The fisherman was swept away. The woodchoppers were never found; but one of their axes was finally picked up a mile and a half from where they had been smoking their pipes. The herd of reindeer vanished in the twinkling of an eye. When the bewildered herdsman climbed out of the shallow well that had saved his life, he found himself in the midst of a charred and smoking world; he was scorched and penniless, but alive.

He had been within three miles of one of the mightiest explosions ever recorded on earth. Something weighing thousands of tons had exploded into a great ball of seething fire that climbed into the clouds in a matter of minutes, leaving below it a stunned earth that sent its quivers to seismographs in many lands.

World War I spread even greater havoc of a different sort and scientists almost forgot the strange explosion in Siberia, which they had assumed to be some sort of huge meteorite. It was not until 1927 that a scientific study group reached the scene. They found a scorched and barren spot that showed plainly the effects of incalculable heat and pressure; trees brushed flat to earth for miles around the center of the blast, their trunks charred by its remarkable temperature. They found a few witnesses, including the herdsman and the man on the river bank, and some villagers who had seen the catastrophe from a vantage point miles away. After examining the scene and interviewing the witnesses, the scientists went away. They had determined that something from outer space had struck in those lonely reaches of the Yenesei, something that scorched and blasted —but something that left no craters in the earth to mark its collision. For want of a better name it went down in the records as the Tunguska Meteorite, and there it remained for more than thirty years.

A Russian scientist, Dr. Alexander Kazentsev, was a member of the Soviet team that spent considerable time investigating the scene of the Tunguska explosion. Like their predecessors, they were puzzled by what they found and puzzled even more by what they did not find. No craters. No logical, acceptable explanation for the recorded fury of the explosion.

Fortunately for science, Dr. Kazentsev was also a member of the Russian team that went to Hiroshima to study the effects of the atomic bomb which had obliterated that hapless city and most of its people.

Dr. Kazentsev was particularly impressed by a peculiarity of the blast; directly beneath the center of the airborne explosion the tops of the trees had been snapped off, while the trees remained standing. Somewhere, he had seen something like that before—but where?

Suddenly he remembered. At the scene of the "Tunguska Meteorite" in Siberia! Tree tops snapped off in one area, while for miles around the trees were brushed flat to earth, just as they were at Hiroshima! But that phenomenon was known to be a characteristic of only nuclear devices. Did it mean that a nuclear explosion had taken place over that lonely Siberian terrain almost half a century before?

There was a relatively simple way to check the suspicion. If the explosion had been nuclear, there would be radio-activity in measurable quantities in the earth. And Ka-zentsev knew that when Professor Kulik had made the original investigation of the Tunguska blast in 1927, no check had been made for radioactivity; he also knew that Kulik had been disturbed by the complete absence of mete-oric fragments.

A new expedition, headed by Professor Liapunov and including Dr. Kazentsev, was dispatched to the scene of the so-called Tunguska meteorite. They spent months track-ing out the radioactive pattern in the soil that sent their Geiger counters chattering; they interviewed an eye-witness who still recalled vividly the great ball of fire that rolled into the heavens and the strange mushroom cloud from which it stemmed. They dug up tons of soil to collect a scant handful of metal fragments. Then they went home to evaluate and study what they had found.

Dr. Kazentsev and most of his colleagues came to the conclusion that some sort of atomic-powered device of tre-mendous size had exploded over the earth at an altitude of 1.2 miles on the morning of June 30, 1908. He calls it a space ship.

In his official report filed with the Soviet government agency which directed the expedition, Dr. Kazentsev says that the blast damage and the radioactivity charts enabled the scientists to locate the point directly beneath the blast and to trace out the familiar atomic cone. Sifting the soil around the edges of this "cone" produced tiny bits of metal, some of which were not of any known meteoric nature and some of which seemed to be alloyed. The eyewitness accounts all agreed on the seething fireball and the mushroom cloud, which we now know to be characteristic of nuclear explosions. And exhumation of some of the long-dead residents of the area indicated that they had died of a "strange malady" indeed, for they were victims of excessive radioactivity.

Says Kazentsev, "The weight of evidence clearly places the explosion slightly more than (a mile) above the center of the destruction. The damage is identical to that produced by man-made atomic devices under similar conditions. The lingering radioactivity, the mixed metals, the descriptions of the explosion itself all coincide with an atomic explosion.

"Whether we approve or disapprove, we must admit that the thing which was long known as the Tunguska Meteorite was in reality some very large artificial construction, weighing in excess of fifty thousand tons, which was being directed toward a landing when its atomic engines exploded.

"This evidence is to me indisputable proof that on that distant day we were visited by intelligent beings from some unidentified origin in space. That their trip ended in tragedy was incidental; for exploration is only deterred by tragedy, not stopped. Having come once, we must expect them again, perhaps under happier circumstances.

"In the catastrophe along the Yenesei river in 1908 we lost a guest from the universe."